regime 02

a magazine of new writing

regime
books

Regime 02: A Magazine of New Writing
Contributing Editor: Andrew Burke
Editors: Peter Jeffery OAM, Nathan Hondros, Damon Lockwood &
           Chris Palazzolo

Published by Regime Books in Australia, 2013.
First Floor, 456 William Street, Perth.
www.regimebooks.com.au
www.twitter.com/regimebooks

Cover image:
Untitled
by Joanna Wolthuizen
(2012, Acrylic on Canvas, 152cm x 102cm)

ISBN 978-0-9874821-0-5
ISSN 2200-7822

CONTENTS

Shane McCauley

Salmon

spawned with its twin targets
instilled —
duplication   death —
harrowed by implacable
journeying

from an ocean's core
up into brief light
effort beyond
mere muscle
mere desire

each neuron on fire
alone
in this striving
its frantically exuberant
living
in this end
is its beginning

Geoff Page

Dear Mum and Dad / I hope you are well

is how the template ran,
those Sunday nights at boarding school,
nine words to get us started.

But what was there to say?
Nothing that could be much mentioned.
Cold sheets, cold floors of changing rooms,

the sleetiness of football fields
or catches missed in cricket,
the boxing tournaments in which

I'd last the first round only.
That happy formula they gave us,
I sensed its sheer fatuity —

though that is not a word I knew,
aged ten. The health of both was fine.
My mother, it turned out that year,

had still one more of us to bring,
closing out on seven.
There was a 'wellness' *there* at least.

My father, just on forty,
had thirty years or so to go
before the cancer took him.

And what could I put down as news?
A test result or two perhaps,
providing they were not unworthy.

A favourite subject might be cited —
though hardly Maths where rattan worked
its miracles of long division.

No mention of the prefects either,
their sadist's smattering of power.
Allusions to a hobby

might fill a paragraph,
leatherwork or crystal set.
A friend or two might find a sentence.

For some years now my addressees
have been much less than 'well'.
I have the timbre of their voices,

their maxims in my ears,
but all of it's from memory only
and ashes in the soil,

soil that's in the family still,
softened under rain.
You could say every line I've written

has been what I could not say then —
the clarities of indirection,
the whisper of the not-quite-said.

I'm back there at that desk again,
fountain pen and letterhead,
my Parker filled with Quink.

If I were less than half agnostic
I still could murmur them,
nine words, and find some extra meaning.

Even here, and even now,
they wouldn't be entirely futile.
Dear Mum and Dad,

I hope you are well.

Kate Middleton

Globe

Grand
Junction
Item: Sagittarius Navigator's Globe, replica   Step up
to see the way the world was shaped, read the names that
covered the globe—this country: *Apaches*   This fracture of
water and future road rising out in empty space, draining
into the *Mer Vermaille*   Step up because

the earliest maps show a miracle, the earliest
            maps flow *up*stream—first

charting what is known
            then crashing into

*the
unknown*   blank space   the unexplored
                            as cartographers gently lap
                                    and nip

at, the land of dreams, spinning
riverine threads out of castaways'
tales

            Beyond the waters—

beyond the black-rocked canyons
and red-rocked canyons

            —somewhere out there

rumoured   lay seven cities of gold   Cartographers pan
Cibola
            across river and land
                    land awash with myths of riches

Rosalee Kiely

What the Crack lets in

Ring the bells that still can ring
Forget your perfect offering
There is a crack, a crack in everything.
That's how the light gets in.

Leonard Cohen

the plum or not the plum.
but not the crimson skin, the give of skin
the tang sweet filaments cling to stone
the plum stone laid on china.

the memory or not the memory.
but not the taste of ashes, writing a name
in ashes
and not the carbonic grief of ashes
the loss of arms, chest, dwelling.

the road or not the road.
but not the seat by the road
the dirty, weary limbs tapping time
and not the splendour and sickness for home
the driver saying God bless our souls.

perfection or not perfection.
but not the well water rising in one vent
and not the breath
and not the trust in hair or music and not
crying by the line, sink, bed
and not the grace and not the courage.

Andrew Burke

Unintentional Art

In sunshine on grey cement
songlines of silver dots
tell a nomadic story criss-
crossing and dotting their way
to their own stringless music

I back down the drive
my wife in her flowing caftan —
purple against jacaranda blue —
waves her arms between the gates
like Phillip Glass conducting

but the music I hear is Cage-like
a gentle marimba of dandelion heads
playing in the grass centre of our drive
beating and twinging on drive shaft
muffler and axles

My wife jumps in at the gate and says,
'Now, we mustn't forget the bank.' Then
turns to me as I fidget: *'What are you doing?'*
'I'm notating our drive, y'know, like
Percy Grainger did with piano rolls.'

Ryan O'Neill

The Martyr

Cochrane kicked the halo from Jesus' head, broke off both supplicating arms, and threw the statue onto the bonfire. Then he sat down on the long, damp grass, drinking from the bottle at his side, and watched as Christ burnt amongst a dozen small crosses. The smoke arose, thick and black, and when his neighbour leaned over the fence and asked him what he was doing, Cochrane raised the bottle to him and said, 'I'm trying to elect a new Pope.'

After searching through the rest of the house, he found only the baby Jesus, and a plastic donkey. The fire had died down, so he took another drink from the bottle, and started toward the shed to fetch some kerosene. On the way he tripped over a *pieta* hiding in the uncut grass, and fell on his back, his glasses flying to one side. He lay there for a moment looking at the sky. The clouds were round, very white and motionless in the dark blue, the sun streaming behind them. Cochrane couldn't move. He felt as if he were trapped in a stained glass window.

'Mr Cochrane,' a voice said. 'Are you all right?'

He sat up. A girl stood in front of him. She was twelve or thirteen, with a wide, plain face and severely cut brown hair. Despite the heat, she wore a long skirt, down to her polished shoes, and a long-sleeved white blouse buttoned to her neck. Cochrane wondered why. She had little to be modest about.

'Who are you?' he said.

'My name is Bernadette. Bernadette Thomas,' the girl replied.

As she spoke her tongue nervously touched her lips.

'I knew Mrs Cochrane. She was my English teacher. I just wanted to say how sorry I am.'

Cochrane started to get to his feet. The girl held out a hand to help him, and he saw that she was deformed. The hand was small, like a newborn baby's, the fingers rounded and barely an inch in length. Though he had taught at the same school as his wife, he didn't know the girl. He got up without her help. She knelt down, picked up his glasses, and gave them to him.

'Thank you,' he said. He saw with annoyance that she had left two greasy fingerprints on the lenses.

'I know it's sad, about your wife,' Bernadette said. 'But really, you should be happy.'

'And why is that?' he asked, replacing his glasses.

'Because she's in Heaven,' the girl said, her tongue darting to touch the top of her teeth, as if searching for the last fragments of a communion wafer. 'I used to meet Mrs Cochrane at the church. I go there every day. And so did she, before... And we would talk.'

Abruptly, Cochrane turned away from the girl and went into the shed.

'We talked about God, and Jesus and everything,' the girl called after him. 'And you, of course.'

Cochrane emerged with a yellow jerry can of kerosene.

'She said you didn't believe,' the girl said. She scratched her check with the malformed hand.

'You don't need to worry,' he said, unscrewing the lid of the jerry can. Then he stopped and tried to smile at her. 'You're too young for all that. Go and play.'

'I'm the same age as Mary when she had Jesus,' Bernadette said defiantly. Then, reaching in her pocket, she said, 'Please, take this. It's a Mass card.'

She stepped back from him. She had smelt his breath, and he saw her look at the overturned bottle on the grass.

'Thank you for coming,' Cochrane said, snatching the card from her.

She had just noticed the blackened stump of Christ in the remains of the fire, and the broken, charred crosses amongst the ashes.

'What are you doing?' she cried. She knelt down in front of the fire.

'I'm tidying up the place,' he said. 'Burning some rubbish. You'd better step back.'

He threw some kerosene on the fire. It whooshed and blazed dangerously for a moment. He lobbed the baby Jesus into the flames, and watched him burn.

'That's blasphemy!' the girl cried behind him. Cochrane kicked the donkey into the flames and said, without turning round, 'It's the Reformation. Ask your History teacher.'

He waited, pouring kerosene on the flames from time to time when they died down. When at last he turned round, the girl had gone. He tossed her card into the fire.

Cochrane had taken compassionate leave from the school for four months after his wife died. When he had cleared the house of all the icons and crucifixes, his drinking tapered off. A few of the other teachers came to visit him from time to time, but he felt nervous around them, like a truant.

It was a hot summer. The sun shone as if it meant there to be no more nights. Cochrane soon forgot about the girl, Bernadette, until one evening at the start of December, when an urgent knocking at his door disturbed him. He looked out the window. The sky was cloudy, red spears of sunlight making tears in the grey. The scene reminded Cochrane of the inspirational photographs Christina used to buy, the kind with a trite, encouraging motto printed on them. He couldn't make out the figure standing on the veranda. When he opened the door, it took him a moment to recognise the girl. Her bicycle was leaning against the wall behind her and she was still wearing her school uniform. He wondered how she could ride a bike, with her hand.

'Bernadette, this isn't appropriate…' Cochrane began. He had already half-closed the door, when he saw that she was bleeding. The blood ran down her ankles, and had soaked through her white socks.

'What happened?' he said, stepping forward. 'Did you fall? Were you hit by a car?'

The girl shook her head, and smiling slightly, without taking her eyes from his, she reached down and began to lift up her skirt, showing her large knees and fat, bloody thighs.

'I was riding on my bike,' she said quietly, 'back from choir practice. And the bleeding, it just started.'

There were in her eyes, as she whispered, 'Is it… Is it stigmata?'

'What?' Cochrane said. 'No! No. It isn't.'

Bernadette dropped her skirt, her large mouth open. She began to cry, and to his shame, Cochrane felt only disgust. He looked away from her.

'It's alright,' he said. 'I'll call your parents. They can come and pick you up. What's their number? Bernadette? Come in the hall, I'll get you a towel.'

He hurried to the bathroom, but when he returned with the towel, she had left. Cochrane fetched a hose and washed away her blood from the doorstep. When he thought of the girl's face he felt like he had killed something.

One day, he finally felt strong enough to sort through his wife's papers. He went through her old textbooks and lesson plans, finding comfort in her handwriting. In the bottom drawer of her desk, hidden underneath some old calendars, Cochrane found an exercise book. He was about to discard it, when he saw the name on the front: Bernadette Thomas. He opened the book and began to read the essay on the first page, titled, 'My Hero.' The girl's handwriting was very small, and neat, and deeply indented in the paper. She had the habit of numbering each paragraph, like a verse in the bible. There were many spelling mistakes, which his wife had corrected in red.

'1. My hero is your husband Mr Cochrane, the biology teacher. He was my saviour when I was being beaten by Josephine Waters from 4C.

2. Josephine hit me for no reason when I tried to give her my lunch money, because everyone knows she is poor and Jesus says to help the poor. Josephine said, 'Are you calling me povo?' and everyone laughed at her, but not me, I didn't.

3. Then she started to hit me. She slapped me on the left cheek, and my nose was bleeding, then I turned to offer her the right cheek, but Mr Cochrane was there, and he stopped Josephine from hitting me again and sent her to Mr Jolley, and though I said I forgave her she was suspended.

4. And Mr Cochrane wiped away all my tears, just like God does. He is a true hero.'

Cochrane could remember the incident now, how he had found the two girls rolling across the hopscotch squares, one pulling the hair of the other, whilst a mob of children screamed and jeered around them. Though she wasn't hurt, it was Josephine who was weeping, while Bernadette smiled, one side of her podgy face filthy and scraped, and her nose bleeding. He had taken the two girls to the office and then forgotten about them. He wondered why Christina had never shown him the essay. Perhaps she had known it would have embarrassed him. Glancing at the next page he saw the title of another essay, 'The 7th Commandment.' Cochrane closed the exercise book and cast it on the pile to be thrown out.

The following day he went to school to see the headmaster. Ian Jolley had always reminded Cochrane of a character in a children's book, in that he resembled his name.

But when Cochrane found Jolley at his office he had a different, worried expression. 'I'm sorry,' he said quietly when Cochrane came in. 'I'm so sorry about Christine, as you know.'

'Thank you,' Cochrane said.

He took a seat. Jolley said nothing, waiting for him to speak.

'Ian, I think I'm ready,' he said.

'To do what?' Jolley asked, tensing in his chair as if he were about to stand up.

'To teach again,' Cochrane said, and Jolley suddenly smiled and settled comfortably again.

'Of course,' he said. 'When do you want to come back?'

Cochrane spent the rest of the week preparing for his first lesson, on Monday morning. He felt nervous when he finally entered the classroom. The students were all sitting quietly at their desks. They were a good class. He had taught them before. But they knew about his loss, and were shy of him at first. He began by making one or two weak jokes, as he drew a plant cell on the board, and the students carefully copied the diagram into their books. He was settling into the lesson, when after twenty minutes there was a knock at the door.

'Come in,' Cochrane said.

The door opened and Bernadette entered.

'Yes,' he said.

'I'm taking this class, sir,' she said.

Someone groaned, and Cochrane looked round sharply.

'That's fine, Bernadette. Find a seat please.'

There were three empty seats, one at the back of the class, and two together at the front, facing the teacher. Bernadette took the desk in front, resting her schoolbag on the desk. There was bright blue sticker on the bag which said, 'Don't let Darwin Make a Monkey out of You.' The girl put her hand up.

'Just wait a moment, Bernadette, and I'll tell you where we're up to,' Cochrane said impatiently. But she stood up and turned to face the class.

'As you know,' she said, in a quavering voice, 'our teacher Mr Cochrane suffered a great loss recently.'

'Sit down, please, Bernadette,' Cochrane said.

She didn't look round, but clasped her hands together.

'I think we should say a short prayer —'

'Sit down!' Cochrane said again, loudly. He was afraid his voice might break, like a choirboy's.

'— to welcome him back. Our Father, who are in heaven...'

Then she was praying for him. Cochrane didn't know what to do. Some of the students had already begun to join in. A group of boys at the back of the class giggled and slipped swearwords into the prayer. The Our Father seemed to last a decade. Cochrane stood still in front of the class, looking down at his shoes. At last, at the mumbled 'Amen,' he said quietly, 'Now, please sit down, Bernadette.'

The girl smiled at him, then took her seat. Cochrane turned back to the diagram on the board. He became distracted, and he knew that he had lost the interest of the students. He felt not as if he were teaching, but giving a sermon. He had to keep two boys back for detention. Despite all the disruption, Bernadette watched him closely, making neat notes from time to time in her book, like his recording angel.

The rest of his lessons did not go well.

He called in sick the next day. Jolley was very understanding, and told him not to rush things. At odd moments Cochrane did, in fact, feel nauseous, and he believed this was when the girl was praying for him. He had begun to feel as if he were one of those pitiful people he would sometimes read about in newspapers who saw Jesus everywhere — in the play of noon shadows from a fencepost, even in a half-eaten cheese sandwich.

In the morning Bernadette went past his house on the way to school. She had a thick blue rope, which she had tied to her deformed hand, and she was trying to skip up and down the street. She was clumsy, and the rope kept striking her on the back. To Cochrane it seemed as if she were flagellating herself. When she had gone past, he went out, intending to go to the school to pick up some marking. He felt too unsteady to drive, and so he walked, taking a short cut across a park near his house. As he crossed into the shade, he stopped. In the distance, amongst some broken swings, a group of schoolchildren were chasing someone across the grass. Some of the boys had stones which they threw at the fleeing figure. Cochrane was about to shout out when he recognised her. It was Bernadette. He stepped back behind a tree, and watched as one of the stones caught the girl on the back of her neck, knocking her down. As she fell, she turned her head. When she caught sight of him, she smiled. Cochrane didn't move. The group had caught up to her now, and some of them hawked and spat on her, whilst others kicked her. One girl ripped the buttons from her blouse to reveal a white, braless, flat chest. Bernadette's face shone with tears and saliva. The bullies had not seen him, and Cochrane said nothing during the five minutes they abused the girl, mocking her hand, her ugliness, her God. Bernadette's eyes never left his, even as they began to close up and blacken.

When her tormentors had finally tired of her and ran off, Cochrane walked slowly up to the girl, who lay on the beaten grass. She opened her mouth to speak, but Cochrane held up his hand.

'Don't,' he said. 'Don't forgive me.'

Then he turned and walked back towards his home. At the edge of the park he looked back, to see the girl standing still in the same place, watching him, as if tethered there by her shadow.

When he got back to his house he sat down first on the couch, then on the floor, then at a stool in the kitchen. But every chair felt like a chair in a waiting room. Finally he sat at his desk. Bernadette's exercise book, on top of a pile of papers in the bin, caught his eye. He opened it and read again the essay she had written about him, 'My Hero.' Then he began the next essay, 'The 7th Commandment.' His wife had only corrected the mistakes in the first paragraph.

'1. The 7th Commandment is a very special one of the 10 commandments. Some of the others are you shall not steal, murder, covet wives or asses.

2. Last week I saw the 7th Commandment. It was Wednesday and I was going to choir practise but I forgot my bag. I had left it in English class, because I was so upset because Mrs Cochrane said that she was ill and would have to take some time off and she is (you are) my favourite teacher.

3. It was 6 pm, but I thought that maybe the school might still be open. The front doors were locked and the back doors were too, but I ran round to A Block and there was one opened door there. I went inside, and went to my English classroom.

4. Through the door window I saw Mr Jolley fornicating with you, Mrs Cochrane. I have met Mrs Jolley and Mr Cochrane, so I knew you were both breaking the 7th commandment, and possibly also "Thou shall not lie."

5. I wept.

6. I ran away from the school and went straight to church and prayed to Jesus to advise me. And now I know what you must do.

7. Mrs Cochrane, you shall not see Mr Jolley again. You shall go to chapel every day and beg God for forgiveness. You shall have God in your

heart and in your house and I will watch to make sure. You shall not tell Mr Cochrane, because he is my hero and he shall not know that his wife is a whore of Babylon. You shall do all this, or I shall tell your husband myself.'

When Cochrane looked up from the book, he couldn't see clearly. It seemed that Bernadette had left her fingerprints on his eyes as she had on his glasses. Outside, the sun had come out, slanting spears of light through the closed blinds, pinning him to the desk. A sweat had broken out in prickles on his forehead, like a caress of thorns.

Kathryn Hummel

Fish on Monroe

She didn't have much of a voice   *but then*
it wasn't much of a band.
Fish in his taste agrees but plays
the record,he hints   just to please me.

Strings swell and burst
The voice coos,climbs to its
staggering vibrato   and carries us all
bye-bye baby
eyes diamond-hard,above all

Didn't have much of a life   but then
it wasn't much of a world   ,still
there are enough
tatters and tassels   rows of slanted lashes and
bottles of cotton wool
there were books   of course
and those numbers   35-22-35
encircling her tomb.

Her voice spins floss between his ears,his eyes
follow the vinyl:
Here is cheesecake beneath the needle.
Skin skin skin   Marilyn tried to cover
with the sedate slip
of her intellect.

The record fixes her incandescence
against red velvet   a jewel
in a cardboard sleeve.
Without the pop picture,he says
he'd never have bid for it.
Even music has a skin to misread.

Mikaela Castledine

The Sea is Theoretical

Some way inland
the sea becomes theoretical
a mad refutable idea
that the land should end in such a way
falling into liquid and into a footless distance
and then that it should be undrinkable

Heretical too
a persistent rumour of gods and monsters
a faint tang revolving around the earth
especially when your travelling takes you
to where
it shines like a smelting pour on the horizon
and could be heaven

The sea is mythical
until it lies before you
alive and flapping as any injured creature
into which you have thrown your stones
a vast and mucused thing
that in your horror and distress
you spear with a long stick
while it shrinks back
again and again.

so you leave it there
returning inland
as a saviour or a scientist
jabbering like a drooling fool
or holding to your story
weeping salt tears
as evidence

Andrew Burke

Untitled

It is an unusually vibrant purple and is valued for its colour as
it neither flowers nor fruits. I don't know

its name. A rapidly moving, but always on the same track,
line of ants moves through and under its spreading foliage,
throwing no shadows in its purplish reflection.

They don't know its name either. Yet all experience it the same.

Karla Linn Merrifield

Into Durango

It's dusty down toward the end of the line.
Raucous, daredevil mountain whitewater,
the aspens trembling in its wake and
strands of snow still clutching peaks,
have given way to dust devils and trailer parks,
lone ponies in bare half-acre lots.
It's hotter far below those Alpine reaches,
where lie misplaced golf courses,
suburban lawns and the tame, blue man-made ponds
at 'The Ranch — Durango's Greenest Acres.'
From squalor to nouveau riches in a few clicks
of steel wheels on rails into Durango. I've arrived.
Dusty, I said, and now add: dry.
Why do they need to irrigate the 19th hole and the
other 18 and each neighbor's yard and garden?
I've been a stream flowing.
I'm not ready to evaporate, not ready to turn to dust.

Roland Leach

Kalahari

It takes a while to die from a Kalahari
Bushman's arrow. Two hours for a steenbok.
Eight for a large buck antelope. Three days
for a giraffe. A slow poison boiled from the ngwa
caterpillar to the texture of red jelly.
It is a slow death. Sometimes tribesman track
for days. And it is then. Couched beside
the dying animal they must experience
death. Lay their head against the duiker's side,
its waning pulse. Crying when it cries out,
shuddering when it shakes. You cannot take a life
carelessly. Life is dangerous but not sad.
You must stroke the head of the eland
with the hand that killed it, the dangerous heart.

Erin Kelly

We, The Boys and Girls

Jane

'Why are you crying?' I lean down and put my arms around her. She is heavily made up and in a short, dark red dress that only she could wear. Her lipstick is smeared and her mascara is gone. She shakes her head and nuzzles into my hug.

'As your all-knowing best friend I will restate my recommendation. You need to forget about him,' I say. She lets out a wail and holds up an envelope. I snap it from her hand and take out the photo inside. It's Marty. With a girl.

'What? Who is this? Where did you get this?'

'It's Marty.' She sobs.

'No shit. Who's the girl with her hands on him?' She just shakes her head, doesn't know. 'Well where did you get it?' I say.

'He sent it to me.'

'Who?'

'Marty.'

'Marty sent you a photo of himself and his new girlfriend?'

'Yeah,'

'But I thought *he* broke up with *you*?'

'He did,' she says, defeated. Suddenly I understand how dangerous this game can be.

'Jesus', I say and take my hands off her, afraid to be too close to this obliteration.

Anna

'Can you believe this?' I say, the next day at coffee with Anna. She looks at it and shrugs 'So what? They aren't fucking.'

'But he broke up with her. I could understand if he was trying to get even, you know. But why would he want to hurt her?'

'Because he's just like the rest of them. This photo is, like…it doesn't surprise me. They are capable of much worse. Considering they were together for years she should think herself lucky.'

Anna has been like this forever. It's not like she's got some sad story, where her boyfriend fell in love with her mother or something. She hasn't been burnt. She was born this way. She just doesn't see the point of wasting time with guys.

'You really still believe all this?' I say.

'They will do one of two things. They either fuck you, and it can feel good. You might even come. Or they will fuck you, and if you want to know how that feels, go ask Jane.'

'What about Dane? He treats me well,' I say, and can't ever imagine him making me feel like Jane. Though I can't imagine him making me come, either.

'There are no exceptions,' she says, and looks at her coffee.

'There are good guys around. You're just a cynic. I'd say it was a gimmick if I hadn't known you for so long.'

A waiter delivers coffee to two old women at the table next to us. He stands to chat for a moment. 'Take this guy,' I say, 'talking to these older women. Cute. You're marginalising people like him.'

'That's Max,' she says, 'He got caught with a woman in the bathroom, an older lady, like those ones, while on shift, two, maybe three months ago.'

'What? How do you know?'

'My cousin works here, remember?' I look at the guy. He seems too innocent to be with anyone other than himself.

'So what's wrong with that? You've never had sex anywhere other than a bed?' I say.

'Well,' she says, smiling, and I know already I've lost the argument, 'at the time he was dating the manager here. She found them.'

'Jesus.'

'The only reason he kept his job was because she left. She couldn't be here anymore.'

Then, 'Also, this Dane character you've been seeing…' she says, as if she hasn't met him several times in the last few months, '…Elle, it's a matter of time.'

Dane

I go home and know I should study and not watch TV. I decide to go to Dane's place instead, both because I don't want to feel guilty about not studying and because I want to know if he is going to break my heart. He takes a while to answer the door and while I stand there and wait I can't help but imagine him having sex with old ladies. But when the door opens and he smiles and says my name I know Anna is a deluded extremist and Jane just got unlucky.

'So what are you doing?' I ask as I follow him into the apartment.

'Ahh…nothing much,' he says as he opens the mail I brought up, pulling open a letter and reading it so intently that I doubt he notices me kissing the back of his neck. I put my hand around him and into his pocket, feeling him, no response.

'Fuck,' he says. 'My rent is going up. Twelve dollars a week. That's, like, hundreds of dollars a year.'

I hug him.

'This is just another hint from the universe that I've been at the bar for too long. I need a better job. Jesus, Elle, can you believe you're with a loser that works a bar and cleans the toilets?'

'You do it with a cool attitude,' I say. 'That's what's important.'

'Yeah, I know. But I need a better job.'

'Well, you could —'

'Jesus, Elle, let's not talk about it. I have the same conversation with my mother each week. I just don't know what I want to do.' He opens the remaining mail and shakes his head.

'I'm sorry, Elle. What were you going to say?'

'I forget.'

'Oh.'

'Do you want to have sex?' I ask.

'Umm…'

'Anyway you want.'

'Nah. I'm kind of tired. Let's watch TV instead?'

'Okay,' I say. *Huh?* I think.

He hands me the remote so I can choose what we watch but I just leave it on the first thing that comes on. We eat chips and soon the volume drops out of the TV, as it often does, and the only sound in his apartment is the crunch of the chips. I feel like studying would be a better use of time than watching a silent TV and eating junk food and not talking to a boyfriend that doesn't want to have sex with me. I think about just leaving, or flashing him a breast and then leaving, but instead I tell him about the photo, and what Anna thought of the photo, and what Anna said about him, how he'd fuck me over.

'The photo is a cheap shot,' he says. 'Tell her to send one back of herself, naked, just to remind him of what he's missing.'

'No way. That's how your parents and boss end up seeing you naked after he makes a thousand copies and plasters them on every telegraph pole in a five kilometer radius.'

'Yeah, you're right.'

'What do you think of what Anna said? About how you're going to break my heart, because that's just what guys naturally do, like growing facial hair.' I straighten up and face him, needing to be assured, needing him to promise he'll never do it. But he just shrugs and says 'Anna is bulimic.'

'Anna wasn't making a personal attack on you.'

'And I'm not making a personal attack on her. I'm just saying, you sure you want to be taking advice from someone who has a psychological disorder? It's like this time I got talked into seeing this band that I'd never heard of. This guy, he worked at the bar for a few months, he told me how he'd been really depressed, and, you know, suicidal, and how his doctor recommended he check into this place, basically a mental institution, and he did but had to check out two days later when he found out his health insurance wouldn't cover it, and I knew all this about him but nonetheless I spent my money and went to see this band. And you know what, it was a wannabe eighties glam metal band with two synths hidden at the back of the stage. I mean. Elle, it was terrible. That's when I truly understood how sick this guy was. But too late, I was there and I stood through the whole ninety minutes of it.'

'That's a long bow to draw,' I say, 'associating Anna, who, yeah, vomits food, with some depraved freak who should be under close monitoring at a mental health care facility.'

He laughs, 'Still, he was a nice guy.'

'Will you say that after the guy takes a gun to my uni campus and starts shooting the place up?'

'I think he'd rather use a knife.'

'Is bulimia even that bad?' I say, 'I mean, I know girls, and boys, party people, who drink so much that they vomit two, three, four times a week. And usually they are in such a state of intoxication that they vomit on themselves or other people, or in the middle of clubs, or in taxis, unlike Anna, who I am sure is very civil about the whole thing. She'd be clean and hygienic and always flush the toilet immediately after. Should we be looking at it as a valid weight loss strategy in our increasingly obese society?'

'Elle, the vomit isn't the issue. Yeah, stomach acid will strip the lining of your throat and stain your teeth, but breathing in carbon dioxide is bad for you, and staring at a computer screen for hours doing a uni assignment actually kills brain cells, so everyone is always ruining themselves. It comes down to the fact that it's a psychological disease. So I would say, yeah, bulimia is a negative.'

The television sound suddenly fills the room and it's a woman moaning, reaching climax. It's an actress who became famous from a home sex tape scandal and it's an ironic case of art imitating life imitating art. It makes me wonder again why we aren't having sex and then I realize that he hasn't assured me or promised me anything and all I've got out of him is that Anna's problem is wrecking her really nice teeth that her parents paid thousands of dollars in orthodontic work for.

'I've just realised I need to be studying,' I say. 'Walk me to the door?'

He opens the door and leans down and kisses me goodbye, tells me I have beautiful eyes and it makes me ask 'Why aren't we having sex?'

His eyes grow wide and he ducks his head out the door, checking the hallway. 'Jesus, Elle.'

'Well, is something wrong?'

'No.'

'Then why didn't you want to have sex?'

It's the first time I've seen him embarrassed.

'I, um… because I jerked off just before you arrived. Sorry.'

'Oh. Okay.' I smile. 'Bye.'

The door closes behind me and I feel like skipping down the hallway but don't. I constrain myself like a grown up would, but grin like a maniac all the way to my car.

Jamie

'Have you ever spoken to someone,' Jamie says and the edge of his lips curve into a smirk, 'and the next day they kill themselves?'

'Eww. Jamie, I came to look at your paintings, not hear about your weird fetishes.'

'Elle, you're such a prude.'

'Maybe compared to you.' The paintings he has shown me are bad, but I tell him they're good. I've known Jamie for as long as I can remember because our parents went to pre-natal classes together. Now his mum is gone and he hates his dad so I guess he feels like I'm the only family he has left.

'Do you, like, get it?' he asks. We're in the middle of his empty apartment and looking at a series of three works leaning against a wall. Dark greens, purples and grey smeared on what Jamie says is the best canvas you can buy. Standing here it seems like a bit of a waste.

'Well? Do you get it?' he demands. When I don't respond he leans his head over in my direction as if I might have a different view. 'Of course you don't get it. You're not arty.'

'I'm arty.'

'You're as arty as an "I love my job" accountant who plays Sudoku all weekend and watches The History Channel.'

'No, I'm arty in the way I live my life. I have my own creative interpretation of life. Some would even say that I'm a great thinker, maybe even cool.' I laugh.

'Not me.'

'Well then, what am I supposed to be getting? Enlighten me.' He turns to walk into the kitchen, shaking his head.

'You shouldn't laugh,' he says, 'It's not a joke. I'm serious.'

If I didn't feel sorry for him already I do when he says: 'Each piece stands alone to tell a story but together they convey the tales of lost souls, ever searching for truth and meaning in a world that has given up on them.'

'Oh,' I say. 'Cool.'

'Yeah,' he says, 'that's generally the response.'

'So people like it?'

'No. It sucks, doesn't it?'

'No. Well maybe a little. Maybe try focusing on something a little simpler.'

'Like what?'

'I don't know. Things that other artists focus on. Love?'

'You think that's simple?'

'I guess not.'

'Jesus. How the fuck would I paint love?'

I sit on a beanbag at the edge of the room and notice a hole smashed in the window. A chipped piece of brick is lying in front of me. Broken glass is scattered across the floor and I guess Jamie has just been walking around it. He probably thinks it's artistic. I don't mention the photo because Jamie and Jane never got on so well. The last time I brought her here she said: 'Just because mummy and daddy aren't home doesn't mean you can smear shit on the wall.' It got her banned from all of Jamie's future art exhibitions. I watch him gaze at his works, wondering where he went wrong. Jamie wouldn't hurt anyone, other than himself.

'So, have you ever seen someone smiling and the next day they kill themselves?' he asks and I roll my eyes.

'No. Why?'

'Oh, I've just heard it's a bit of a trip.'

Mum

I speak to my mum that night because she likes to hear about Jamie. I tell her how he has dedicated his life to a painting and that his paintings are terrible.

'The last thing that boy needs is another disappointment. After what happened between his mother and father.'

'Well he was talking about suicide,' I say, and smile to myself as my mother begins ranting about young people and drugs and death.

'I know, I know,' I say to her, 'I told him just to keep it simple. Paint *Love*.'

'How on earth could he do that?'

'I don't know. I'm not the painter.'

'Elle, you might have rose tinted glasses about love now, but it's not what you think.'

'So I've been told.'

'Honey, love is mathematical. If you want to search for true love in seven billion people, you'll be looking all your life. You'll know you've found the right partner when you determine that the expected quality of all previous and future matches is lower than your current partner, based on an analysis of personal traits and lifestyle preferences. Taste and money matters more than all this nonsense about soul mates.'

'Oh. But that's so...cold.' I can't believe what I'm hearing from my own mother. She used to write poetry. I wonder if it's because of what happened with Dad. I say I'm tired and that I've got to go and she says something about 'love and war' as I hang up. All I can think about is that I don't like mushrooms, which are Dane's favourite food. Fucking mushrooms.

Marty

I see Marty the following day.

'Elle, how are you?'

'Well, I'm about to get my heart broken over mushrooms, and you're a dick.'

His eyes widen and he suddenly looks like a little boy, incapable of the destruction of my friend. 'Let's get some coffee?' he offers.

'Okay.' I say, 'You're buying.'

We find a shop and order.

'So why'd you do it?' I say, good friend, bad cop. I fold my arms.

'I'm sorry that Jane is sad, of course I am, but Elle, it's like what Bob Dylan said, when something's not right it's wrong. I didn't feel like there was a reason for us to be together anymore. Maybe I could have treated her a little better toward the end there, like that night where I told her I didn't think she was as smart as me, and that all the books and music and films she likes are made from a formula designed for fourteen year olds with too much pocket money. But it was over a long time ago. Why waste anymore time? And it's not like she was innocent. She tried to convince me my grandfather was gay, and that if we were to ever have kids we couldn't let him see them. I mean, what the fuck? The night she got really high she told me she dreams of her ex-boyfriends all the time. She told me she was bored with sex but then refused to try any new positions. The list goes on. I've been over it all in my head. It had to end.'

'So you sent her that photo because she wouldn't try new sex positions?'

'Photo?'

I dig it out of my bag and place it in front of him. 'The photo you used to destroy my friend. You might as well have paid Mike Tyson to take a swing at her. It would have hurt less.'

'*The fuck is this?*' he says.

'Like you don't know.'

'That's not my photo. It was taken at the zoo. On Abby's camera.'

'Who is Abby?' I ask and he points at the girl in the photo. He becomes tense and I don't want to say anything.

'Abby sent this to Jane?' he stares at the photo in disbelief.

'I'm sorry, Marty,' I say.

'For what?' he snaps. 'The fact that Jane is hurt and that I'm being charged as a sociopath, or that my girlfriend is the sociopath?' It's strange hearing him say 'my girlfriend' and not be referring to Jane. 'Why would she do that?'

'Marking her territory,' I offer, and I realise Marty, and Dane and Jamie all need to be afraid too, not just us girls.

He slumps back in his chair and sighs. 'You think you know someone. Shit.'

'Yeah,' I say, and wonder what Dane is doing. I chew my nails. 'It's like, you know when you see someone smiling and the next day they kill themselves?'

And he says, 'Yes.'

And I say, 'Oh.'

Jake Davies

On finding a dead girl in your bathtub

1. Offer to make her a tea, bring her a blanket and compare bruises.
2. If she's in burial dress, complement the white lace cobwebs.
3. Don't ask too many questions. She will find talking cumbersome and is prone to fatigue.
4. Listen to her when she does speak — even if she's still a child, she knows more than you.
5. Her means of communication might not be immediately intelligible, but remember:
   a. Blinds are words
   b. Light is meaning
   c. Birds are commas
   d. Inaction speaks loudest
6. Don't be deliberately coy, confusing or 'enigmatic'. People spend their whole lives not understanding each other, and she's the better authority on this.
7. The dead are usually reserved, but there are gestures common to most. Definition follows description.
   a. Tears off an earlobe — *'Nobody cares how clever you are if you have nothing to say.'*
   b. Depresses the cheeks — *'Your friends needn't be pretty, but they **must** be beautiful.'*
   c. Rolls her eye in her palm — *'Cynicism requires no effort and even less talent.'*
   d. Pushes teeth through lower lip — *'Your life is a dress rehearsal. Jeer yourself from the wings.'*
   e. Pressing her thumb to her wrist — *'While you're asleep, time goes through your pockets.'*
8. Don't ask her about the afterlife. She is in your bath. She doesn't know.
9. She may have acquired a twitch at her time of death,

particularly if it was sudden. Tell her it's lovely and
cultivate your own.

10. It's likely that all the books you've lent out will be flung
onto your lawn during her visit. The dead attract the
dead. Read her the one that breaks the garden gnome. It
will be her favourite.*

> *Unless it's post-modern: 'Post-modernism
> laughs at funerals.'

11. At some point, she will ask you to turn on the bath's
taps. Run warm water. Fill a cup first if the pipes are
cold.

12. After she has dissolved, be sure to keep your head above
your heart. Sleep upright, bound in curtains.

Peter Jeffery

For Juniper

As one newly emerging in the expanding, exploding discovery of art,
I had interviewed Juniper one of our three best —
Even then, fifty years ago, close to classic
And already suspended in Swanland's gallery,
For us to revere until this year and beyond.

And all I remembered of that late sunblast afternoon,
Was myself skipping, stumbling or was it sliding?
In a criss cross fashion
Down a steep Darlington hill,
Totally primed, sublimed on Bob's White Burgundy —
Like him, considered the State's best.

Re-entered into that afternoon, by his sudden passing,
I can only think of a sun shower,
Compacting rich red earth, and bringing granite and gravel, and quartz
Into bright patinas of small indents of water,
All on an ever diffusing canvas from rich oil to fading pastel,
With a feathering carpet of dried and falling leaves
Cast against the great Kalgoorlie serpent pipe,
Buckled windmills and sliding wooden mine heads,
Making all in its half moistness, half dry
The red, the dust a gentle canvas of patterning delight.

And now in a flash it is all past,
But I will remember until I too pass,
The searing sunblast,
The cooling sweet smelling sunshower
That was Juniper
For me that long gone afternoon and ever now.

Glen Phillips

from Kandimalal: 4 Wolfe Creek Poems

4. A Walk Through the Crater

To the Djaru this sacred
circle formed where the dreamtime serpent
descending here
left its entry debris,
the next creek that
to burrow towards
needed to be formed.
We stepped down
boulders of shale balls,
fused iron oxide,
and slid steep slopes
to the crater's floor.
Followed a faint path
towards the epicentre
and a straggle
of spindly scrub.
Ramparts all round
of this open eye
staring back, blindly,
to a crescent moon
and beyond to where
cosmos gave it birth
those three hundred
thousand years before.
If we waited long enough,
the evening star
might pass close to glimpse its offspring's grave.
We circle once and climb back before
the crater blinks.

About Wolfe Creek Crater

Situated over 130 Kms south of Halls Creek and the Great Northern Highway, Kandimalal (or Gandimalal) meteorite crater was first mapped from the air in 1947 but was well known for thousands of years to the Djaru (or Jaru) and Walmajarri people. It lies some 22 kms east from the Tanami 'highway' which leads past the area and through the Tanami Desert and on to Alice Springs in Central Australia.

The crater is nearly 900 metres in diameter and the 'walls' or rims rise about 60 metres above the crater floor. After the 50,000 tonne meteor's impact at about 15 kms per second, some 300,000 years ago, the crater was about 120 metres deep but most of the meteorite material dissipated as an explosion leaving a few scattered meteorites up to four kms distant and much pulverised local quartzite and laterite. Shay balls of iron oxide also were formed by the impact. A small clump of salt wattles, roly-poly and paperbarks has grown up in the crater's centre.

Such meteor impacts should occur about once in 25,000 to 50,000 years. The pillar of fire in the Bible (Ex. 13:21-22) was the night-time pathfinder provided by God for the Israelites fleeing from Egypt. It is also linked to the descent of the Lord to earth (Ex. 19:9) in the theophany at Sinai.

The Djaru people's legends of the formation of the crater tell of either a close encounter between the new moon and the evening star causing the latter to impact with the Earth, or that the crater was formed by the dreamtime rainbow snake (or snakes) emerging or going underground at this point after forming nearby rivers or creeks such as Wolfe Creek, Sturt Creek and Halls Creek. The area is now a national park.

Glen Phillips, 2012

Rodney Nelson

Drunken Lines at the Wrong Party

Rainer Maria Rilke teaching in the

Dylan Thomas dividing his time between

Robinson Jeffers being named fellow of

       try to imagine all that
       and point me home

Charles Pitter

Literary Correspondence

That cool summer, Charles wrote letters to Ginsberg, Kerouac
Mailed to San Francisco and Lowell with no hope of reply
Ginsberg, dead — Kerouac, dead
And the dead don't often reply to literary correspondence, do they

High on San Francisco T, a postal clerk responded on behalf of Allen G
Ablaze with chat about City Lights, and where the Beats used to hang
The North Shore, 29 Russell Street, 1010 Montgomery Street
Nope, they weren't there anymore, but you could take a tour, and hey
Write back, care of the Golden Gate administrative bureau

Meanwhile, Kerouac's letter was endlessly re-directed from State to State
The USPS had him down as staying with his mother, but she was always
        on the move
Not bothered much about literary correspondence
So much as her cats, and her darling Ti Jean, Jack
Kerouac

Geoff Page

Seven Births Are Seven Deaths

How often did she think about
the old man I would have to be
to see her wishes granted?

At the end her seven kids,
mostly in their sixties then,
had managed somehow to survive

the vagaries of gravel,
the cancer genes, the wayward hearts
and all the accidents by turn

a station life can offer.
For those of us who had to leave
she wished a job in town,

a marriage too (and happy mainly),
a pension (in good time),
a house to raise the child or three

who at the end might see us off.
Flood-grey in my early thirties,
I must have spooked her just a little.

Did she see me stooped already,
the vaguer side of eighty,
tilted on a walking frame

with three soft meals a day?
She had no time for such addresses
and vanished via a heart attack

the night she entered one.
Being protestant and prudent,
she must have done some thinking though.

How old were we in her mind?
I think most probably the ages
we'd been when we were children,

roaming paddocks, riding ponies,
clambering on rocks
or all day in the seaward pools,

that carefree '40s/'50s childhood
before the marital progressions,
the wash-in of the grandkids with

their varying degrees of charm.
Eighteen in all she had
but none of them displaced her seven.

Our futures and their limits though
must be our own concern.
She always knew that she'd be gone

and so would never need to see
the slow varieties of decline
or unexpected ends

the life she'd given us required.
Seven births are seven deaths.
Beyond her nineteenth century maxims,

she never talked about it much,
hoping maybe that, like her,
our timely fadings from the frame

or swift obliterations
would likewise guarantee that we
don't see what happens to our children.

Christopher Konrad

The Voyeur

1

How thick and black her hair.

All this time she has walked past these bronze gates. All these years I have never really seen. She might as well have been a ghost: an apparition, like all mankind to my blind eyes. Eyes I have blinded for Him.

2

Why does he not look at me? He walks past and, for all he knows, I might not even have drawn breath. Strong eyes. Glasses, but that's a sign of an intelligent man. At least that's what my mother tells me. He always carries a briefcase: a paper under the crook of his left arm. I get the feeling he is well read; that he has travelled and knows the world, but does not know I am in it. He wears a dark brown homburg hat, the colour of a rich coffee, set slightly on an angle, though not jauntily, and a long liquorice-green coat. He takes long, confident strides and when it rains he always holds his umbrella straight up. The sign of a man who knows what he wants. But who does not want me.

I do not know why I care. I do not know this man at all, yet something inside my arms itches, like a hair shirt, when he passes by. At nights I look out my window across to the big factory chimney stacks, flumes for smoke cut into angular pieces by the beams of the large industrial lights, lights bigger than my living room. When I look out there I see my unwanted future.

My sister disappeared last month, like all those others: so many young women. We all know what happened to them. We all know they lived in a splintered hell before they died, horribly, but we block this out. If we didn't, we would never leave these *barrios*, never leave these dusty, blood-littered streets, nor would we go down to the waiting, murdering buses that take us over to our other hells, the sweatshops. My heart has collapsed like the Mojave Desert. I cry quietly into the sweaty air of the

Juarez night when I think of her suffering I know but deny, which my sister has endured. The other girls here act tough; they smoke and drink and make hard with the boys. They tell me to harden up and to get over it, to get over myself; what makes me so special? Harden up girl, or you will end up like your little sister.

I have not seen the man in his homburg hat for over a year now. Maybe he was a businessman who had finished his work for the day. Perhaps he too was taken away by the cartel men and had his throat slit. Maybe he was a writer. He *looked* like a writer who had simply finished his story and left because there was nothing else left to write.

3

The two women found a quiet part of the beach to get changed, far away from severe eyes; hung up their towels on a limestone ledge, donned their flippers, goggles and snorkels and swam gently into the settled, crystal-watered bay. They stayed there forever because that is what people in love do. They feasted on simple acts that pass from day to day. Every now and then they took a break climbing onto a small flat reef, breathing in salt, seaweed and wind; taking in the horizon that wove around them like a mantle, confirming their love. Back on the beach, walking towards their clothes they spoke about the tranquillity of the place, the sinking evening blue. I could not tell whether they were lovers or sisters. Does it matter? Love is.

4

Fra. Anthony: You must surely not be reading all those errant works, Fra. Thomas. They will lead you to no good and destroy you as so many before you.

Fra Thomas: It is not what goes into you but that which comes out of your mouth that defiles you, Fra. Anthony.

Fra. Anthony: Still, better men have been broken. Look at how heavy a fall a giant like Meister Eckhart can take! Now he is a heretic. I implore you, Fra. Thomas. For the sake of Christ.

Fra. Thomas: I am reconciled with myself. I am pure in the eyes of the Lord.

Fra. Anthony: Arrogance, Thomas. Pride, as you well know, before perdition.

Fra. Thomas: Christ is who we must celebrate, Fra. Anthony, not live in fear.

Fra Anthony: I saw you with her again last week. There in the back field; where the mill is. I *know*, Thomas.

5

It was Rimbaud who wrote that it was not his fault that brass wakes up to find itself a trumpet.

Philip K. Dick, self-purported madman, visionary and drug-addled writer, had much the same idea.

PKD had an obsession with dark-haired girls to the extent where he put together a collection of poems, essays and letters called *The Dark Haired Girl*. This girl might have been a particular archetype for him. Perhaps a Freudian analyst would have traced back the beginnings of his obsession to some maid or some other maternal type in his infancy, when his own mother was busy abandoning him.

This girl is of the dark end of the spectrum of light. This tells the enquiring reader much of what he or she needs or wants to know about the author of such a book. This girl is mysterious. The adjective 'dark' conjures up a sense of 'out of the light': perhaps in shadow. She allows the author unlimited imagination, since it is in the unilluminated region of the brain where many unforgiveable things are hidden or sequestered. This also imparts to the obsessed an air of innocence. For example, the author might claim *I did not know I thought those things; it is not me, it is someone or something else that creates these thoughts; this is my dark side wanting to express itself*, and so on in a similar way as with Rimbaud: I am not at fault; I am not in full control of these desires, urges, thoughts.

She is dark-haired from the more temperate regions of the world, the Latin or Mediterranean or island regions. This allows him, the author of such a text, a sense of vicarious adventure or adventurousness through her; she is liable to take risks to which other, lighter-haired girls are not inclined. Or so he thinks. But so much more is conjured up if he positions the girl as dark, of the darker side, the chthonic side of life.

6

K.D. sings 'Hallelujah' at the 2010 Vancouver Winter Olympics. She brings the crowd both to their ecstatic ovation and their metaphoric knees; thousands out of their seats. She makes people cry.

•

Renee sat in a bar at Antwerp. Even *she* had forgotten where she came from, but she remembered that she had a major in English Literature. 'Please forgive me' read the note as she walked out of his life forever.

•

It was August 1980. Hanna was merely an eighteen-year old girl who had lived all her life in Andalusia. She started having sex at fifteen and already knew one hundred and one ways how to make a grown man groan like a woman, even when he was bending over her, thinking it was he who had the power.

•

There were many Canadian girls travelling through Tasmania back then, in the same year that he was. For some reason, they were mostly blonde and fun-loving, and they mistook him for your average hormone-filled young man. But he was reading *Peter Camenzind*, a *bildungsroman* by Herman Hesse. Like the protagonist of that novel, the young traveller was in search of himself, in the wilds: searching for poetry, searching for a reason; for what? Before *Camenzind*, the traveller had read Hesse's *Glass Bead Game*. He was a follower of the great German-Swiss author, and studying how to become an anchorite. There was no sex for him in those bush-dance days of the southern regions around Franklin. The girls left in search of other available young men. He returned to his own town on the West coast to look after his elderly father (just as Peter Camenzind had).

7

She had seen him, through those unusual bronze gates, tending the garden in the many times she had walked past on her way to work. Sometimes she caught him looking up at her but quickly turning away as she turned towards him. She thought he was good-looking, in a plain kind of way, but, because her passing-by took place over so many years, his face became very familiar to her, like a husband's face to a wife of many years. She had never married and had only the occasional boyfriend, but none of these flirtations led to anything serious. She wondered what it would be like to dedicate oneself to God in the way that this man had. What effect would seeing a young woman waltzing by freely, as she had done for so long, have on a young man like him.

8

She lit up, drew in hard and the cigarette glowed like a demon. The smoke swirled around her like a winding ghost, an emulation of a soul leaving a body. The tendrils of blue ether remained woven through her hair which was black as pitch or ebonite, wrapping around her arms like protective velvet armour. With the same hand that held her cigarette she picked up her whiskey. She treated the drink, as with most hardened drinkers, like a close lifetime friend. The truth was that she had never smoked until a year ago and only started drinking several months back. She had been an entirely different person before all this.

A man in a finely cut suit sat himself next to her as if this were his natural and rightful place in the world. She chatted to him as if this were her purpose in life. Now. His tie was silk and dark puce. His beard closely trimmed and grey, matching the colour of what little hair was left on his head. Almost like a cliché, he must have been around sixty years old. She was twenty five.

9

It was only after they laid him deep in the dirt that I knew the meaning of forever. No, not then; it was when they draped the multi-hued flag over his coffin, a rainbow cloth, even before it went into the ground, that I knew for sure that it doesn't matter a damn if a person is a she or he, they or them or even an 'it' that cuts the cloth of the human in us. It is how you die. He died with great dignity, but more importantly, with happiness. What matters is whether you can play with life, with what is given, and if you can say goodbye in compassion for those left behind.

10

How many can start with a fortune?

11

It had been weeks since I last saw her, but yesterday she came by again. I only saw her for maybe fifteen seconds, maybe twenty at most, as she whisked by the gates again and again and again. I know what time she usually comes by, perhaps on her way to work or study, every morning. I place myself there, by the gate, deliberately, just to get that glimpse. But yesterday it all changed. She looked over and saw me watching her, and she smiled. This was not new, it had happened in the past, not many times, but nevertheless it happened. What was different yesterday, what changed everything and now I know I cannot stand at the gates and wait for her anymore, was that she spoke.

The possibility of her is now lost to me forever.

Michelle Faye

Blowie

Davey trailed behind his older brother Tom as they followed their father and two uncles across the stretch of beach. They walked in succession, like ants, or soldiers marching out to war. The older men balanced rods across their broad, bare shoulders and the tackle jingled and click-clacked with every step. The sun was close to setting and they had to reach the bay and set up their gear before they lost light.

He was a lanky kid and usually light on his feet but the men were moving fast so he was forced to take leapfrog steps to keep up. The men's footprints were large, deep holes in the wet sand and with every step he tried to land each of his own footprints into theirs. His brother appeared to be doing the same thing and, although he was taller than Davey, even he appeared to be struggling. He could see the crack of his brother's bum beginning to appear out the top of his boardies. Looks like it'll be a full moon tonight, he thought, and laughed remembering all the times Tom had said the same line whilst dacking Davey on their driveway, in car parks, at Woolies, even on the school oval one time.

They were the kind of brothers that mucked about like that, gave each other a hard time, but always had each other's back. At school last term a year seven boy was shoving Davey around, scabbing for money for the canteen. He kept tugging at the straps of Davey's bag, trying to yank it off his back and throwing him around in the process. Davey was on the verge of squirting some tears when suddenly, from nowhere, Tom's at his side swinging his own schoolbag into the year seven's head with all the force of a superhero and screaming, *Here, check my bag ya dickhead!* Tom ended up getting a weeks detention for that one but the kid never bothered Davey again.

He watched his heroic brother now, skipping ahead of the men with his ratty unbrushed hair lopping from side to side as he chased seagulls from sand to sky. Tom was two years older but Davey often felt like the more mature one. Today was his tenth birthday, and their father had insisted on taking them fishing. Although he and Tom usually loved all the same things: Footy, Cricket, Playstation, BMX bikes, Tekken III and Batman over Superman any day, Davey wasn't really a fan of the beach or fishing. It was kinda boring and the bait was icky and made his fingers smell fishy for days. But he saw the whites of Tom's eyes grow big when they overheard their father that afternoon.

I'm gonna take the boys fishing later.

His mother had come into his room and made a point of asking Davey if it was what *he* actually wanted to do.

'Course it is!'

His father at his mother's side spoke for him. She flinched, unaware that he had been there, but still waited on an answer from Davey himself. Tom had been behind them in the hallway, hands together in prayer, silently pleading and nodding. Davey felt put on the spot with all six eyes on him, so he feigned excitement.

They reached the groin of rocks just before the sun disappeared behind the water but not without leaving its mark on the sky. Patches of pink, red and orange swirled together like fairy floss. After dumping the gear Davey and Tom headed straight for the cliff and began to scramble up it in search of rock-pools to explore. They came across rubbish mostly. Cans, broken beer bottles, lots of cigarette butts and what appeared to be a used condom, before being beckoned by their father.

'Boys! Nah! Get down! You can wait til' the tide goes out a bit.'

Davey and Tom shrugged their way back down the rocks.

'After I've had me first catch I'll show ya's how to bait a hook, orright?'

Their father wore a cap pulled so far down his face that you could barely see his eyes. It was rare that he would look you directly in the eye anyway and Davey had become accustomed to talking to the rim of his father's cap. He had been told by his mother on several occasions that he had his father's eyes though he wasn't sure if that was a good thing or not. His father had a quick temper and if you did manage to catch his eye it could sometimes feel like peering into a dark, shadowy tunnel.

'Can I cast out for ya dad?'

Tom was hopping from foot to foot trying to get his father's attention. Davey watched his father put a Winnie Blue to his mouth and light it. He chucked the pack into the esky and scooped up his rod all in one swift motion, then headed out into the water without saying a word.

For some time Davey sat still and ran his fingers through the sand, watching his old man down at the waters edge, calf deep in the dark waves. Everything seemed silent and still except for the white water battering the shore. Now and then his father would call out to Davey's uncles and they'd all laugh. They were gradually becoming silhouettes, shadowy figures against a painted backdrop in which the stars began to slowly show their winking faces. Davey created a pillow out of his father's red fishing jacket and sunk himself further into the warm sand. He breathed in deep; the salty night air mixed with the smell of Lynx, cigarettes and Bundaberg and made him think of home. His mother would be in their yellow kitchen drying dishes, her thin hands always moving, or maybe on the phone, crying to some unknown person on the other end of the line. The small black and white television that sat propped on two VB cartons would be blaring the 'Home and Away' theme song and muffling the cries of his baby sister Ashley who would be red faced and snotty in her highchair, wailing for her freedom.

Davey awoke to rain on his face, his eyes springing open to find his brother leaning over him dripping seawater from his straggly hair.

'Look bro, boobs!'

Tom had been playing around cutting up ocky bait and making pictures out of the black ink that spilled from their goopy limbs. His fingers were black and his teeth flashed as he grinned.

'That stuff stains ya know?'

'S'if I care. Look what I found in the esky!'

Tom was holding a navy blue stubby holder in front of his crotch and swinging his hips, making humping gestures. Davey blinked hard. It had a picture of a blonde woman lying on a beach with her breasts out.

'Think chicks like this come to Rockingham?'

Tom was still dry humping her face. Davey shrugged and looked towards the water. He wasn't sure how he felt about it; she just looked cold and uncomfortable to him.

'Maybe we should get Dad to take us to Swanbourne next time.'

'Huh?' Davey was beginning to feel cold and uncomfortable himself.

'Swanbourne…the nuddy beach. Geez mini D, I needa teach you some things ay.' Tom chucked his stubby holder girlfriend at Davey and it bounced off his knee and rolled down the sand towards the water.

'Good one.'

'Jynx!'

'Oh well, maybe she'll end up at Swanbourne where she belongs.' Davey joked, but Tom had already lost interest and was now poking about in the esky and intermittently throwing sideways glances over his shoulder.

'What're you doin?'

'Nothin'. Let's go up the dunes.'

Before Davey had time to respond, Tom's back was already to him and he was halfway across the beach.

'Davey! Come on ya pussyyyy!'

Davey scrambled up and legged it after his brother.

The sand was cool beneath Davey's feet and the air felt colder up on the dunes away from the warmth of the gas lamps. It was dark, so dark he could barely see and the lights from the coast road that flickered further up in the distance were too far to illuminate the sand hills. He could hear the sound of waves crashing on the shore and the distant hum of traffic, but otherwise the silence was as ghostly as the dunes themselves. Goosebumps began to rise up his forearms and he shivered from the cold, or fear, or his sudden need to pee.

'Tom?' His voice came out in a broken whisper.

'Tom? Where are you?'

No answer. Great. With every step, rough saltbush branches scratched at his legs and he was sure his right calf was bleeding. This was a stupid idea and Davey felt himself starting to panic. His eyes began to well up like that day at school when the year seven had picked on him, but he willed himself to hold it together and stop being a bloody pussy. He was ten now and ten year olds shouldn't be afraid of the dark. Tom wasn't. Tom wasn't afraid of anything. He took after their father that way. Hard as nails.

Davey bent and tried to examine the damage to the back of his leg, but it was pointless in this light — *toughen up mate* — he heard his father's voice in his mind. He was about to turn back when he noticed a shadow over on the dune to the left of him. He paused and squinted, trying to make it out, it was probably just a saltbush. Yeah, just more shrub with cat claws for leaves, but something about its stillness unnerved him. He squinted again. Was it growing bigger? No not growing bigger, moving, moving straight towards him! It was getting closer but Davey's legs wouldn't go, he was stuck, he could hear the thuds of its step in the sand, could hear the rise and fall of its breathing.

'Tom? Is that you?'

Davey's heart was pounding in his chest, it was beating too fast, he could hear it in his ears, his legs began to feel like jelly, he turned to leg it back towards the beach but something had a hold of him, was grabbing his arm.

'Helloo Clareeeece.'

Davey let out a girlish scream that bounced off the dunes and sounded even shriller in the open air than it had in his head. Tom's face suddenly appeared out of the dark, his chin, mouth and nose lit up in an orange glow. He was holding their father's Bic lighter beneath his chin and smiling creepily.

'Gotcha!'

'Fark...' Davey was still trying to catch his breath '...you!'

'You scream like a little girl.'

Tom was using the lighter to inspect the ground before finding a clear patch of sand between the scrub and sitting down. The flame kept going out and every few moments they were plunged into complete darkness.

'I'm going back.'

'No don't.'

Davey could hear Tom shaking the lighter fluid, before his face appeared out of the black again. He sat down opposite his big brother and drew his knees to his chest in an effort to try and keep warm but in that moment he felt very aware of himself; of his girlish scream, his close call with tears, his skinny, scratched up, jelly legs that nearly gave out on him. His father and mother were always arguing: He needs to toughen up, no boy of mine is gonna — He just has a delicate nature — *acts like a fucking girl.*

He pushed his legs back out from under his chin and sat with them apart the way Tom was sitting opposite him, chucking a spready, elbows on knees.

'So...what now?'

Tom fumbled around, one handed in his coat pockets, before pulling out a crumpled cigarette.

'Birthday present.' He grinned.

'Where'd ya get that?'

'Esky. C'mon, let's try.'

Davey watched as Tom put the wrinkled cigarette to his mouth and lit it, the same way their father did. Puffs of smoke hung like cobwebs in the night sky. He thought again of home and his mother who would be trying to put Ashley down with bedtime stories. Fairies that live in gardens or sleeping princesses in castles, waiting on kisses from dashing princes. He secretly wished he were back there, in his blue room, snuggled beneath the Batman doona, under a ceiling of glow-in-the-dark solar systems and drifting off to sleep to the sound of their mother's soft, gentle voice.

'You try.'

The end of the cigarette glowed red as Tom extended it to him. Davey's reluctance to take it made for a clumsy exchange and he burned his finger and dropped ash on his boardies during the process. He could hear Tom clicking his tongue as he tried to hold the creased fag between his thumb and index finger the way he had seen their father do, before sucking hard on the end.

'Shit mate, you orright?'

Davey was keeled over, spitting, spluttering and coughing like he'd swallowed something down the wrong hole. His chest tightened, he felt his lungs cave inwards and his throat felt overcooked.

'Shh! Stop coughin' up ya lungs for a sec. Think I heard summin.'

They paused in unison, like rabbits listening for danger, ears pricked, wide-eyed and motionless. Their father's distant voice carried up to them.

'Shit!'

'Jynx!'

Tom quickly pocketed the lighter throwing them back into darkness and within seconds Davey felt his brothers sandy hands yanking him by his arm roughly to his feet. The sudden jolt made him dizzy. The moon had emerged in the sky as if from nowhere and was now spinning above his head, the stars danced and blurred together and his chest still hurt as they scurried over the dunes, dusting themselves off and racing one another back towards the distant glow of the lamp.

Their father's rod jerked about as the fish on the end of his line gasped for sobs of air. It was white with a shiny black cape covered in yellow spots. The waves crashed at Davey's ankles as he stood at the water's edge and watched his father reel in his catch. Tom was doing cartwheels on the sand, throwing himself around in excitement.

'Good one dad!'

Their father swung the line towards Davey and, as he did, the fish began to blow itself up like a balloon. A balloon covered in tons of sharp, pointed spikes.

'It's jussa blowie ya morons, don't get excited.'

He tilted his head towards the bobbing fish.

'Davey, grab the gloves and get this thing off my line would ya?'

'Me?'

'I'll do it dad!' Tom already had the oversized gloves on his hands.

'Nah, Davey can do it.'

'I can't dad.'

'Tom give Davey the gloves! Fucksake.'

Davey's hands were swimming in the gloves and they shook uncontrollably as he neared the ballooned-up fish; their father had lowered it to the sand and it now flapped and jolted about, starving for air. Its every jump caused Davey's heart to spasm but he felt the pressure of his father's eyes on him. After three attempts he finally managed to catch the fish beneath his left glove, but as he felt for the hook the fish twisted in his hand, a spike piercing the glove, and he spilled backwards wailing. His palm began to throb. He could hear his uncles laughing and suddenly imagined picking up the dumb blowie fish and ditching it at their fat heads.

'Christ. Tom, show ya brother how to be a man would ya.'

Tom took the gloves from Davey and dislodged the hook from the blowies blood-specked mouth in a matter of moments, then handed the fish to their father.

'Watch this boys!'

He flung the fish into the air in front of him then dropkicked it like a footy out into the night sky where it slipped away silently. Davey found himself wishing he could follow the blowie, he imagined walking out across the water's glistening surface, following its path to the moon, and slipping silently into the black water, never to return. He stropped back up the beach and watched moths butting themselves at the gas lamp instead. Tom was still down at the water's edge, picking up shells and kicking them out to sea the way their father had booted the blowie. Even though he and Tom were so alike, there were times, like this one, when they were completely different and it made Davey feel so alone in the world, like an outcast or a superhero that nobody understood or appreciated; like Batman. But if he was Batman, then Tom was definitely his Robin. He sucked at his swollen palm, it tasted of metal and salt and fish, a bit like vegemite, and he cried quietly.

'Davey...' His father's rod was jerking wildly again, 'you're up!'

Davey stood with a sigh, running his fingers through his hair and breathing in a gust of salty air that swept across his face and dried his tears. He sniffed, swallowed hard and headed towards the flash of silver on his father's line.

Robbie Coburn

from **Shadows Off Grandfather**
after Mark Reid

2.

at the greyhounds

somewhere around the bend
where man's eye sees blindness —
a disturbance in the sand.

the dogs bound forward
leaving all work and time
in the grains.

you wait there
commander
& trap your son.

you hold him there
as if your arms
were better years.

Rose Hunter

[umbrellas]

i get the *elote* and he gets the *vaso* and to finish
leave them for the pigeon the skinny one
but the fat one flies up green and purple
hula glistening and here we have it he says
the fat get fatter and the skinnier get   i say
a lion eating corn anyway
can lead to a type of turn for instance   i know it's responsible
for the way he's looking at that girl   and how i'd like to
wear hardly anything like that   seem
hardly anything like that whereas my
little girl schtick   gentle heckler tagalong vibe
along for the ride   i'm too old for it
really   i think to be someone's appendage
                pigeon's wing
if all i can do   is catch him in the flash
                the perfect picture has everything i like about him stop
silver silver with blue trim
welcome to reality it's a painful ride
says big guru lion   *learn how to negotiate* but i say i will not
treat this as a stock deal and do not need to take advice
twenty nine years ago his last shot of dope
invalidated all i will ever say   i was ten
people look lonely when they're walking away alone
although you don't know if they are or not
and worse if they walk slow
i didn't know we were not in the middle actually then all i knew
was that under an unfolding
beach umbrella you were astonishing

Carly-Jay Metcalfe

M.B.

Wearing leopard print
makes you look like
a two dollar whore
who should be on her knees
reciting Bukowski with
wine stained lips.

Haiku

Long tufts of mangroves
wind down river. Gossamer city
with its sheeting rain.

Gary Colombo De Piazzi

Knowing Yourself

If you dare language to read yourself
you may find yourself crumble
under the weight of words.

Words that dissect and interrogate
petty moments, indifferent moods
you no longer cherish

and in the investigation, realise
there is no substance to your days.
Words that strip and bare flesh

expose muscles and skeletal
workings in desperation, loneliness.
How, in all this mass, there is emptiness

that cannot be pinned, a void in the soul
that permeates every cell, every fibre
every motion consigned to the lean look.

Only the brave and imbecile
sift through words. Separating, classifying
categorising back to the essence

the character of individual strokes.
The definition of I.
The ember of all being, the source

of conflagration and desire that draws
and tugs breath to flare the movements
of everyday. Holds the template

against which all encounters are compared.
In the final analysis find humility
and gratitude becomes a way of life

in all the dark and lacking moments.
Those who know themselves
those who know their words
find strength and survive.

Jonathan Hadwen

There is a Stillness

There is a stillness when the fridge's motor whines down
    and the
woman downstairs traps her cough
    in her straining lung
and the chair legs don't scrape
    across the wooden floor
and the birds whose names I do not know
    who do not know their own names
sing a brief song none-the-less.

Paul Fauteux

Camera Obscura

I will die in between things; in silver halide
salts, unfixed. The veil presents as blackened
paper with medial perforation, waves
particles of light as the space permits.
In every glint there is new context, as I
am spilled in pieces onto photo-paper.
There should be a stopper — a thing to close the eye
when I am whole — fit and un-changing.
You're pulling all the bones from me. Enough.
A man is selling pretzels. Winter's thawed,
and park bathroom sinks have running water.
I miss the dog, shitting on my stoop.
You're pulling all the bones from me. I want
to watch the apples coming in. From buds.

Damon Lockwood

The Last Saturday in September

1

Though the cops are here later than normal it still means Julius is in trouble again. I do not sleep very much and I can spot most of the night sounds. The police car is heavier than most cars when it turns up and on to our gravel driveway, crunching like so many dead beetles.

Dad got home not so long ago. He stumbled up the steps a bit when he got home. He will be mighty pissed with Julius again.

Susie is kneeling next to me and we are peering beneath the dining room blinds. We can't see the front porch from here but we can see the front yard. Sergeant Clarkson has left the lights of the police car on and the two front doors open. Sergeant Clarkson is a 'decent bloke' and he always says the same thing to me when I see him on Main Street, near the police station.

'Hey there, Gerry boy, still keeping your eye out for a change in the weather, are we?'

I only do for like the next fifteen minutes after he says this to me but I don't think I have ever seen the weather change. I'm pretty sure I still don't really know what he's talking about.

Susie is one year younger than me but she is a girl so likes to think she is seven years older. I like to say she is my best friend but she doesn't like to hear it. We sleep in the same bed but we can't tell anyone at school and I like the way she smells different.

'Wonder what Julius has done now?' she whispers.

'Something bad', I say.

'Gerard, Jesus.'

I am supposed to be a bit slow but mum says I am the best help in the kitchen she has ever had. Mum has long red hair and wears high heels in the kitchen. Uncle Murray has told me he would like to have a bit of my mum, and I reckon any bit would be just as good as any of the rest, and when I told him that, he sort of greedily agreed.

Suddenly Julius appears behind us from his bedroom door, naked from the waist up. He is grumpy like he always is but he is strong like a barbed wire fence.

'What the fuck's going on?' he complains, rubbing his eyes.

'Julius!' says Susie, the light from the blinds casting pale yellow train tracks across her face, 'why aren't you out there getting into trouble?'

'Why does it have to be me getting into trouble?'

'Because you're always the one doing something wrong', and I get a stiff clip across the back of my head for again stating the bleeding obvious. This always confuses me, because I don't know what else to say apart from the bleeding obvious, but, like dad often says, that really fucking pisses people off.

But Julius has joined me and Susie beneath the blind and they are so close to me I can feel both their breaths. We all have thick brown curls like our dad but my brother and sister 'wear them well' where mine looks like a forgotten mop on a massive head. Julius is sixteen and doesn't care and one day I hope to be just like him.

'What the hell are the cops doing here? I haven't done anything wrong for a month!'

Sometimes Julius smells of cigarettes and sometimes I just want to hug him and my sister but this time he pushes me off because suddenly I realise they both might actually be a little bit scared.

'Gerard, fuck!'

We can hear dad's agitated voice spitting out of the kitchen. It sounds like maybe mum is trying to hold him down or something, or maybe Sergeant Clarkson just spilt a cup of coffee.

I love my family, and we all like the football, though mum sometimes goes out the back with a glass of wine when it's on the telly.

'Who won today, Julius?' I ask, because Julius does know everything.

'1982 VFL Premiers, the mighty fucking Carlton Blues over Richmond by eighteen points.'

'How do you know, Julius?' asks Susie, and I can't tell if she's scared or terrified, but her little fingers are gripping the window sill tightly. Mum says she is a perfect country town princess, the Ararat fairy, if only she had red hair.

'I watched through the window of the pub with Bongo.'

'Bongo,' I say, not meaning much, not meaning to state the bleeding obvious, and he doesn't have brown curls like us, but long blonde hair which makes me a little nervous.

'Watched dad get pretty sozzled, too,' says Julius, who scratches his chest. 'He got into a bit of a blue just after I left as well, apparently.'

'Carlton blues,' I say, not meaning much.

Just then Sergeant Clarkson brings dad down the front veranda steps with his hands behind his back. There is a reflected glint of handcuffs. Susie moves her hands to her lips. Dad doesn't seem to be able to walk straight.

'Fucking hell', says Julius, also jolting back, just like Susie.

'Call my son a imbecile, will he…' slurs dad, and then he stumbles and slams his forehead against the passenger front window of the police car. Dad's hands look muddy, like a muddy red. 'Won't say that no more…' Dad mumbles, or sort of moans.

Mum stands on top of the veranda, trying to move down the steps, but also not. She is still wearing her daytime green floral dress that Susie says accentuates her hips. Susie says that because mum says that, I think.

2

Mum is sitting on a kitchen chair and Julius and Susie are sitting at her feet. Julius is tall enough for his head to be just below her bosom. She is slowly stroking both their heads. Sergeant Clarkson and his police car and dad inside it are all long gone. I am sort of standing around the sink.

'It's really late,' I say.

It is really quiet everywhere. Mum sometimes looks at me. I have red BMX bikes on my pyjamas, and I notice now I missed a button at the very bottom of my top.

Elise Kinsella

The Meaning of a Moment

Of all the teeny-weeny, cute-as-pie, trending-right-now cafés in Melbourne. Of all the cafés with China tea cups, recycled furniture and broadsheet newspapers. Of all the cafés with gluten free bread, more soy than dairy milk and tattooed baristas of indeterminate gender. Of all these cafés, the girl had to walk into this café. The first, and only other time, the girl walked through these doors, one of her life moments played out. You know those moments? Those grand, grand moments that can write a life, that can tell a story, change a story, or even begin a story. The girl had one of those moments right here. Well, she's close to sure she did. The girl has this belief that's been hard for her to ignore, that this moment had secret, life changing meaning hidden within. Standing here now, at the scene of potentially one of her life moments, she is convinced of this conviction. It's just the exact meaning of the moment, it's not quite clear to the girl.

She feels a bit like a thief who has tunnelled all the way to the bank's super important, super secure safe. She's standing alone within grasp of an epic treasure but the password she wrote down on her hand in her difficult to read scribble has run. It was probably her stress sweat that did it. Thinking about it, the girl decides it doesn't really matter what caused this metaphorical ink run, what does matter is the result. The password, the key to her treasure, is largely illegible. It could be used as a guide if she took a really positive attitude. You know the kind of attitude promoted in the Seven Ways To Be Successful at Everything kind of books. The girl doesn't read these books. She sneers at them. But, for a reason unknown to the girl, she does under the influence of this café, feel a determination to piece together the missing parts of her password and crack the meaning of what she is just a sliver from certain was one of her life moments.

The girl sits at a corner table and orders a piccolo. She opens her notepad and writes the headline; 'Emotional Detective Work'. It's time for her to begin. She thinks back to the moment when she was again right here in this café. She's waiting for deliverance from the God that goes by the name of caffeine when another walks through the door. He approaches the girl. His eyes intent. Attempting to discern reaction from the blues of the girl's eyes. 'Can I hug you?' he asks.

He holds his arms out but his hands remain within his shirt and its slightly too long sleeves. Nervously pulling its excess material into little folds. He maintains a slight distance. Unsure. They have spent the previous fifteen hours together, for six of those hours he was asleep. There's a pause as the girl hesitates. Not quite understanding. But then she blinks, and as her eyelids make their usual journey from open to closed and closed to open, the girl can see, just for a second, what is really before her. In front of the girl is a vulnerable man, standing alone, asking to be hugged. And that's when the girl notices the bare feet. The bare feet get to her. Because the girl knows that this man has run down two flights of stairs, crossed The Most Civilised Street In All of Melbourne and chased her here, to this café, with bare feet. The girl nods, accepting the hug.

The man threads his arms through the girl's open coat, shocking her slightly. His hands trace the girl's hip bones. Inside to out. Gently he encourages her body towards his own. The girl notices they're making a scene. Right in front of the coffee machine. Right next to the line to order. Shocking. Awkward, so very, very awkward for the polite people. But they can't look away, are you serious? A man without shoes has started hugging a girl without socks in a most inappropriate way, right here in front of them. They must know what happens next.

A middle aged man is there. He had been pretending to read an email on his phone. A phone, being held in a hand, now hanging loosely by his leg. Already forgotten. The middle aged man is shocked by this couple. It's their ages. The middle aged man guesses at the man's age. He must be over seventy, he thinks. The middle aged man can feel joy, glee and hope, definitely hope for his own future, rising within. A man over seventy is touching a beautiful girl under thirty. And it's consensual. The middle aged man wants this couple to become even more inappropriate. He has seen such things on RedTube. But as the middle aged man imagines where the man can next touch the girl, he becomes aware of himself, an extra, standing in the scene. He is disturbed.

The man himself, the star of the moment, sees no-one but the girl. He holds the girl's body closer and closer to his own, he runs his right hand along the girl's back. He feels each of the girl's ribs, and it makes him fear she is already fading from him. The man moves his left hand to hold the side of the girls face. He feels the girl's shiny, shiny hair, he feels the rounded outline of an ear. The man, through his thumb, places pressure on the girl's ivory white, right cheek, and he is reassured. The girl is here. The man lowers his head and leans in further. He shuts his eyes and rests his temple on the girl's collar bone. The man needs to feel, with his whole being, a single loose strand of his diminishing hair, rise as the girl inhales, and fall as the girl exhales. And he absolutely must protect this glow and crackle that works its way from his chest, out to the extremities of his body, through his shoulders, his elbows, through his stomach, his hips, down through his knees, and all the way to his fingers and toes. But the girl does not know any of this. The moment demands everything of the man. He cannot identify a thought, cannot express an idea, cannot give voice to such a thing. He can do no more than stand and hold the girl and feel all that this moment is.

The girl breaks the moment. 'You've got no shoes on, you ran after me with no shoes.' The man looks down. Had he not noticed? In winter? Impossible. It was something before a thought, before an idea, a something that exists on the edge of either, that had formed within the man and told him in a loud clear voice, 'You can't let the girl just leave.' But now the man does not know exactly what it is that has driven him with such clarity to this girl and this café. He retreats. He turns from the girl and strides past the middle aged man who is still watching, and is now disappointed. Who will take his coffee home to his bedroom, to his laptop with its RedTube. The man picks up pace as he again crosses The Most Civilised Street In All of Melbourne, and panting, climbs two flight of stairs, two steps at a time.

The girl clicks her pen and writes a line in her notepad. This line concerns plot. It reads: 'Café. Girl. Man. Hug. No man. Girl. Café.' The girl is disappointed. She has learnt so little. She remembers what the High School English Teacher said about plot. 'The plot is just what happens.' Or, maybe, thinks the girl, maybe the question of the plot isn't what did happen, maybe it is what didn't happen? Or what could have happened and why it did not?

The girl sips the last of her piccolo and looks at the exact spot a man once asked to hug her, and she wonders, would things have been different if the moment had not been broken? Would the man have found words? An idea comes to the girl. It creeps across her conscious mind and whispers, 'the screaming thoughts that drove the man from you, were but half his war.' The idea goes further. It makes a suggestion. 'The night before the hug, the man's moment, was a battle, an epic struggle, within the man himself.' The idea asks a question. 'And in such wars are there regrets? Life shattering, weepable, lamentable regrets?' The girl has not fought in physical battles. But conflicts designed to wound, to maim, to destroy oneself, these wars, she carries the scars from. The girl nods.

Emboldened, the idea asks another question. 'Are there also wars with victories? Raw, barbaric, conquering victories? Victories that can win the life of another?' The girl pauses to adjust the lens she has viewed the moment through. The idea has taken her to the cusp of something new. The idea asks its final question. 'Do you think the man regrets his victory?' The idea is no longer. It has exploded into a suspicion that the moment was for the man, his victory lap. Of course the man will never regret the moment, the girl finally answers the idea that is no longer. Winning is not a thing we regret, the girl confirms. To herself. The girl writes, 'He came, he conquered, he claimed that which he had won.'

The girl is not sure what to do with her notes. She does not think she has yet found her meaning. The girl can see it's time. She must study the night before her moment. The girl does not really want to think about this night. She has spent a year not thinking about it. Trying not to think about it. But she has no other way of finding her much longed for meaning. She must go on the only way she knows how.

The girl inhales. Deeply. She thinks back to the night before her moment. It begins with a group leaving an underground bar. Slowly students are taking their leave. Are rushing towards tram stops. Are wobbling down the city street on bicycles. Are walking towards an intersection in pairs. The man and the girl are the last two left. 'Which way are you going?' the man asks the girl. The girl points towards her terrace house. 'I'll walk with you,' the man says.

They walk silently. There is an ease to this silence that neither feels the need to break. It allows one to take in the other. The man lets the girl gain a step on him. He traces the outline of her skinny legs, covered in tight black jeans that show her exact shape. He lets his gaze rest on her bottom. He notices its muscles tighten as she takes a step and loosen a she drops a foot to the ground. The girl can feel exactly what the man is looking at. She does nothing to stop him. She would feel silly, breaking his gaze now.

Outside a Dracula themed musical restaurant the girl stops to let its departing staff past. The man takes a step towards the girl. They stand in the shadow of a large sign of Dracula. The sign has a spotlight lighting up Dracula's sharp teeth, Dracula's red lips, Dracula's cape. The man moves towards the girl. He leans into the girl until her body stops against the closed door of the restaurant. The man holds the girl firmly in his left hand. The girl knows the man is married. The girl knows the man is her teacher. The girl knows she will be in his class next semester. She runs the outside of her left hand along the man's cheek. Lightly she traces the outline of the man's top lip. She starts in the left corner. She follows the line of the lip to its first peak. She traces the big dip to the lip's second point. The man catches the girl's finger in his hand and kisses it. The girl does not look to the man's eyes. She can see only his lips. The girl kisses those lips. Gently. The man answers that kiss with a kiss of his own. An urgent kiss. The passion surprises the girl. The energy surprises the girl. She was not expecting this, from him. She pushes back. Matching the man's intensity.

The man kisses, licks, bites the length of the girl's proud neck. He places a hand on the girl's hip. He runs his hand up and up the girl's side. He heads inland. He finds a little hill. He plays on this hill, plays with it, until the girl breaks a kiss to gasp and look at the man in shock. Amazed that the man has done this to her, here. It breaks the man's focus.

He looks around the dark city. He notices a group of teenagers walking up the street towards them. They are rosy from too much beer. Still wearing football jumpers hours after the game has ended. They are re-enacting one of the key plays. The shortest teen in the group runs ahead of the others. He is pretending to carry a football under his arm. The man recognises him. He can do nothing but stare. The footballer feels this stare. He turns to face the man. It is not, the man can now see, his grandson. He releases the breath he had been holding.

The man looks again at this girl. She's in her late twenties but her elfin body, her shyness is more in keeping with the appearance of a teen. The man has been attracted to the girl since the day she stumbled in late to her first class. Apologising profusely. Dropping books and pens. Flustered. The man had wanted to hold the girl's shaking hand and calm her. But his desire has hardened since that day. The man has felt trapped by this desire. It has held him against his will, and he in return has fought these feelings with greed for her attention and a rage against the power she holds over him. The man lifts the girl up and wraps her slender legs around his waist. Thankful he has always maintained his gym routine. That he can still do this. He thrusts against the girl. His hand dives under the girl's top. He rips the girl's jeans open. An urgency drives the man that will not allow him to pause for a second. To end a kiss, to find the button to the girl's jeans.

The man feels for the girl. He drives the girl. Again and again and again. The girl is overwhelmed. The man has taken hold of her entire being. Is in charge of her. The girl wants to know if the man has always been such a lover. And she worries a little at his age. He really is exerting himself. The man notices he has lost the girl. That even now she has drawn within. That he still does not have her. He runs his hand along the girl's jaw. Drawing the girl's face back to his own. But the kiss is a gentle one. He feels defeated.

The man begins to cry. Softly. He's trying to hold back his tears. The girl hugs the man. But it doesn't help. The man begins to sob. The girl stands up so she is facing the man. She leans towards the man and gently she begins to kiss the man's tears away. She starts just below the man's eyes and softly kisses her way down his cheek, over his slight stubble, all the way to his lips. The man tastes his own tears on the girl's lips. The man returns to kissing the girl. He sobs and kisses the girl, tears stream down his face and still he kisses the girl, his whole body shakes but he continues to kiss the girl. The girl steps back. She turns to hail a taxi, holding the man's hand to reassure him. The girl will take the man to a hotel where she will hold the man until he slumbers. But the girl will stay awake. Shaking. Unnerved. She feels violated. She shouldn't feel violated. It was sex. Sex she sort of initiated. But still that feeling is there. It has to do with the intensity of the sex, the girl understands. The man consumed her, stripped her to nothing. The man took all of her. The girl wants to tell the man he had no right to do this.

That's it, thinks the girl. That's what got to me about my moment. About his moment. He felt all that these moments were. He lost himself in these moments and then expressed all he felt. He desired, he chased, he won, he cried. He lived. Wholely and completely, he lived. The girl had done none of this. She had not chased the man, she simply failed to look away. She had been the conquered one and yet it was the salt of the man's tears that had past from her lips to his own. She had taken what was offered. And she had resented what was taken from her.

As the girl sits, her pen poised above her notepad, the café's door opens. She's about to write another line when she looks up to take in the new visitor. It's the man. He orders a coffee, turns to find a table and stops. He has seen the girl. He stands still. In front of the coffee machine. The girl's heart beat speeds up and up. It flutters down to her stomach. It pulses through her ears. She can feel her head move in and out to its rhythm. The girl thinks back to her moment. To its meaning. She thinks about all she has learnt as an emotional detective.

The girl rises from her chair and walks towards the man. She stands close to the man, pulling at the edges of her cape. There are just four words that she can think to give voice to. Standing in front of the coffee machine, she looks deeply into the greens of the man's eyes and nervously asks, 'Can I hug you?' The man nods and the girl gently moves towards the man. She holds the man, clutches at the man, her nails dig into his wrinkled skin, drawing a line of blood to the surface. She flinches as she feels the lust of one for the other. She frowns at the pain she felt when he left her here, in this café. She remembers the taste of his tears and one lonely tear of her own makes a sad journey down her cheek. She laughs, loudly and suddenly at the thought of the café patrons who watched them embrace with such obvious shock and horror. The girls leans in closer to the man, with nails now tinged red, trying to feel all of the man. To be closer to him than is physically possible.

She rests her head on his chest, absorbing his heart beat. Bah-boom, bah-boom, bah-bah-boom. It echoes through her head, it bounces off a shoulder, creates a thud against her hip and shakes her organs, one against another. The girl cannot identify a thought, cannot grasp onto an idea, cannot articulate any of her emotions. The girls stands against the man, clutching at him, feeling for him, breathing in time with him until the tattooed barista breaks the moment, shouting out the man's coffee order.

The girl turns and retreats from the man, from the coffee machine and it's waiting line and finally from the café itself. She looks down at her hand as she closes the door behind her, half expecting the words 'it's about what you feel,' to be scrawled across her white, white skin. The girl laughs at herself. She laughs and laughs from the sheer joy of this moment. She has her precious meaning. But more than that, she knows how to detect the meaning of all moments. The girl feels incredibly rich as walks down the Most Civilised Street In All of Melbourne.

Sofia Chapman

Villanelle: Detention Centre

Write out 1000 times,
now you are in detention:
'I must not enter Australia without permission.'

Il faut cultiver notre jardin.
They try to get us gardening — condescension.
Rye, tout a thousand thymes.

The irony of Broadmeadows. My qualms —
a ville a wood; to glimpse them daring climbs.
I must not enter or stray, leer, without permission.

What of the colour of my skin, my arms
are aching — carpal tunnel. Letters of activism.
Why doubt one, thou send'st alms.

Amidst our prayers in makeshift Mosque, admission:
neath carpet carved a tunnel; bros in arms
I muster not in Australia without perdition.

What of the squalor of my kin, or my intention?
they'd still kick me (they'd call it extradition)
right out, 1000 times.
I must not enter Australia without permission.

Ashley Capes

St Mark's Square

from our train the few towers of Venice
float
as if guarding
the edge of the world,
they hold back all the space
left over from old maps, when the world
just ran out

stopped
in a massive, continent-sized waterfall.
Piazza San Marco is ankle-deep in pigeons

and their leavings,
jazz bands
sneak into the drinks
and coat the yellow
tablecloths

and though we don't sit down

we eventually have to stop,
as people invariably halt
to stare up at bronze, replica horses
and unhook
their jeep-like cameras
right in the middle of the flow

and it is only later when we are on our way
out
that it doesn't
that it shouldn't matter

and the square goes *hush*
as sunlight melts on the Bell Tower
and Gabriel is set to blazing.

Barnaby Smith

Talented Wives

Talented wives
don't usually show
their genius.

Instead preparing
evenings of chicken grease
and powdered milk,

these teachers
of a million souls,
gazing with lustrous heat

upon the brown rust
of that gigantic, obscene
ladle.

Carol Millner

Under the Jacaranda

I.

This I know,
heart's blood — Pohutukawa,
Rata, flowers
red. But what is this —
this fine singing hue, this
Jacaranda? I thought the sky
was blue.

II.

We need new words, said the radio announcer,
words for the new technologies, words for
the brave new world.

But I'm down the garden, I said. Under the Jacaranda.
Besides, I'm not finished naming the old world yet —

Let him stride off, like Burke and Wills, into a
brave new world. All their camels, horses
and cabbage tree hats didn't save them, nor bring
them back to Cooper Creek a half day earlier.

What use was 'DIG' carved into that tree's bark?
What use the buried letter, full of words?

No thank you, I say to the radio announcer
with a wave — You go ahead without me.

I will stay here, reclining, like the Buddha,
wondering at sky and tree — loosening my attachment
to 'purple', 'blue' and 'indigo'; waiting for the next perfectly
strange flower to fall and kiss my bare arm.

III.

Inside this purple globe
one pendant seed pod

swings. Is it disguising
the plurality of winged

black seeds —
new worlds of purple?

Or is this swinging whirl —
this 'O' inside the tree's

own world to be the last
word of all in an ancient

language, we never
really knew?

Ian Nichols

Facing East

Leo Parrish killed himself out at Tamarama Beach, in a cave that he'd hung with real Persian carpets. I'd sat there with him sometimes, all night, talking and laughing and rolling up little balls of hash to feed the fish. We'd throw them out of the cave, down into the rocks below.

I took Denise up there once and slept the night, after the Anarchist Cellar had been busted. We rolled up in one of those carpets, and when we woke up, Leo had come, and he was speeding. He had a giant bag of felt pens, like you can get in Coles, and he was trying to draw the way that we looked to him. People always try to draw on speed, in the morning, when it's hot and your throat's dry and your body feels odd and pissing feels really strange. Leo was giggling because he couldn't get the patterns in the rug right. That was only a few weeks before he cut his throat.

Denise died on the road, ran into a tree on the way to Canberra, a couple of years later. We never really got to know each other, even after we'd lived together for a while.

When Leo cut his throat, he'd brought a whole lot of beer into the cave, so he couldn't have been on anything. He never drank when he was on something. He was always burning his hair when he was stoned, just the fringe part at the front, because of the way that he used to lean forward and hold his head with the same hand that held his cigarette. When I saw him with a crucifix, there in the cave, he was holding it just like he held the cigarettes.

I worked in a psych hospital for a while, and I ran into a couple of people who fell in love. After they left the hospital, cured, they went out into the middle of Centennial Park one night and took a couple of hundred Nembutal each. Real suicides are like that; they look for a place where no-one will find them. Fakers just slit their wrists and show you the blood.

We only missed Leo when Allen Cooper came around, looking for some acid that Leo was getting for him. He waited all night, looking at the mess on the kitchen table and talking about games. He'd already paid Leo for the acid, with some money other people had given him. He came back the next night, looking again. He walked in when *Surrealistic Pillow* was on. We only had two albums; *Surrealistic Pillow* and *Sunshine Superman*. We played them all the time. Someone was always turning them over or changing one for the other. I used to wish for some other records, for a change, but I knew all the words. Even now, after forty years, I know all the words.

We gave Allen some acid we had lying around in the freezer, but it was only a little bit, and he wanted a hundred tickets for the people who'd paid him, so he ate it. He brought out a special that he'd mixed; cocaine, morphine and methedrine in water in a little perfume bottle, one of those you use for dabbing behind your ear. You took out the little stick in the middle and licked it, and that was enough. Gary came around about two in the morning and he had some of those pressure-pack things for chilling beer glasses. We were breathing that stuff out of plastic bags when some guys arrived, looking for Allen and the acid.

When Allen was busted, up in Queensland, they'd put a telephone book up against his ribs and smashed into him through that, so as not to leave bruises. He giggled at them, all the way through it. He told me, 'It bugged the shit out of them, and they got angrier and angrier, but I was still controlling it, they hadn't taken over. It got so that I was coughing blood and laughing at the same time, but they never took over.'

Allen sat these guys down, they were mostly from the University, and started making them cups of coffee and tea and stuff. You could see they were waiting to bust out, to break something. They were all going to be doctors, or lawyers, or something like that, so I suppose they only had a little bit of time to enjoy themselves. One of them, a Med student called Stuart, was really out of it, and kept making animal noises instead of speaking. I think they'd arranged for him to be the heavy. He got one of the people in the house to shave off half his beard, just by making animal noises at him. Neil, he had the bedroom opposite me upstairs, was going to sneak up and knife him, but I talked him out of it.

Nobody knew where Leo had been for the last few days. Leo never had trouble getting gear. He knew everyone, even the old-timers like Peter Collins, who'd been selling dope to jazz musos in the forties and made a fortune selling acid on street corners when it was still legal. Leo wouldn't rip anyone off. He and Allen had known each other for a long time, and they were as much friends as you could be. Leo even knew the mafia guys who hung around the Cross, cleaning their guns and talking about their last hit while they tripped. He could get anything, a hundred tickets would be easy.

Gary had a car, and some of us sneaked out to it about five o'clock. Allen was talking about movies to the University guys and they didn't know what he meant, so they just held their coffee cups harder, pretending they were in control and making animal noises. He was putting them into a movie, and they didn't know it. I think that's the way they functioned, no matter what; hold those coffee cups a bit harder, thrust those chins out and make animal noises. No wonder they wanted the acid.

Black Harry was drinking Muscat, just to keep in character, in the lane behind the Wayside Chapel, and he said that he'd seen Leo. I saw Black Harry in Los Angeles, about ten years later, and he gave me a smile like a stranger. He wasn't drinking Muscat then. He said that he'd seen Leo at the Ship Inn, the morning before. Leo had been drinking schooners and talking to the shift workers just come off and the public servants having a heart-starter before going to work at Garden Island. The Ship Inn opens at six. He'd said he was going to mass from there.

Anna Scott was the only one of us atheists who was willing to go to the early mass, sit through it and stay to ask the priest about Leo. She was a Catholic atheist, and she'd been to St Mary's before. The priest remembered Leo, alright, because he'd put a big bundle of notes, over five thousand dollars, in the plate, and the priest had thought it was a mistake and chased him down the steps. He was a young priest. He said that Leo had said something about clearing up debts and going home.

We picked up Allen, and the University guys just followed along. They were pretty out of it by then; up all night and Allen had been feeding them his mixture, to keep them awake. Stuart was still making animal noises. I don't think they were capable of anything but pretend aggression by then, even though they held their coffee cups very tightly.

The early morning nude sunbathers kept on telling us to piss off as we climbed across to the cave. We only wanted to find Leo.

All the animal noises stopped when we saw him sitting on the Bokhara rug with blood all down his front. He must have died looking out at the sunrise, although that would have been pretty trite. He had Allen's acid in an envelope in his bag.

Later on, after I got married and made it into the educated middle class, I found out that every real Persian carpet has an imperfection in it, so as not to offend god.

Andy Jackson

FDA
(Funeral Director's Assistant)

The officer led us in, like we were picking up
lost property. She was under a rough blanket,
the fluorescent light on her thin arms —

her body curved like a comma, her young,
flat chest covered in thick, dark hair.
I could have picked her up with one hand.

But each body must be carried out by two —
OH&S and all that. The drive back is quiet.
All we ever get is a name and an age. This time

I can't stop picking at the silence. It wasn't
suspicious — her parents took her to the beach
on what they knew would be her last day,

called the ambulance. *It's none of our business*,
my partner says, his eyes on the road
and I'm brought back to the tea-room talk

about *that kind* of worker, though no-one says
if they quit or are sacked. White lines pulse
towards us in the pre-dawn light, the cabin

adrift in the familiar voices on the radio —
news headlines, the same new songs.
If I was younger, this might haunt me.

Joanna Wolthuizen

Listen to the Rhythm

Ben's shirt was stained a darker shade of blue under his arms. He looked dishevelled, and his chest rose and fell with a fast paced rhythm as it struggled to catch each breath. The strap from his satchel tugged his shirt, opening its collar wide at the neck, as Lena stood balancing on the curb in front of him. The street was wet from summer's perspiration and cockroaches scurried, their hardened backs reflecting the street lights.

'I missed you,' she said, her eyes were bright and she held her breath longer to help discourage the show of excitement on her face.

'I missed you more.' Ben replied as he stepped closer to her. 'I ran all the way,' he continued, looking down at his shirt where the darkened patches were spreading.

Lena smiled sympathetically, 'How was work?' she asked.

'Shit,' he replied 'How was your day, did you meet Jules?'

'No, I heard him come in but he went straight to his room.'

Ben gave a knowing smile. 'He's like that. It's not personal. You'll meet him eventually, and wish you hadn't.'

Ben took Lena's hand and they went inside.

The building smelled musty and the carpet was worn down in the centre of the foyer and every hallway from years of work shoes treading upon it. The fabric was grey and hard in those parts and frayed at the edges. It was a grotesque brick building that Ben lived in; the windows were thin and offered no insulation and the glass rattled in its slim frame when the wind was only moderate. The entrance was a mangled version of a luxuriously grand setting with ornate art-deco double doors that stood atop four curved steps, leading up from the pavement. They swung like a heaving dead weight and their tarnished brass pole handles rattled and were sticky to touch. The elevator inside was industrially awkward with its large, non-functioning caging grate that pulled only three quarters down to the concrete coloured carpet floor, which was heavily stained from spills and wet treading.

Ben's flat was on the seventh floor and his bedroom window looked upon the neighbouring building, which was another hideous block of grey rendered brick that simulated a coy looking prison. There were spirals of barbed wire on the rooftop perimeter of that building to deter birds from perching and soiling the façade and Lena thought this strangely pedantic, given the unsightly and decrepit aesthetics of the construction in its raw state. The windows were smaller than those in Ben's block and appeared blackened from grime and neglect, and from their west facing perspective. A narrow passage ran between the two buildings and collected an assortment of oddities which provided a constant stream of indistinct sounds; most of which conjured images of weighted liquid drops breaking open on foil and plastic.

'Jules?' Ben called out as he walked with Lena through his slim hollow-core door.

They waited for a sound to be echoed in reply, but nothing came.

'He must've gone to the pub.' Ben remarked as he adjusted his partially soaked shirt.

'I'm going to grab a quick shower,' he said.

'Ok, I'll meet you in bed.'

Lena walked on the creaking floorboards leading to Ben's bedroom and opened the paint flaked window to let the musty air escape. The street's fragrance was little better, and the air which filtered up from the passage was perhaps equally as musty as Ben's room. Lena undressed and crawled onto Ben's slim double mattress which rested on the floor beneath the window. The worn out cotton that encased Ben's duvet was patterned with a dark and eclectic motif, faded nearly to oblivion and the sheet was maroon, matching Ben's only pillow. Lena moved the pillow to the centre of the mattress and laid her head on one corner. She glanced over the room, which was of modest proportions and contained an old chest of drawers, a writing desk with a rusty wire chair, and a portable piano stood beside the door. There were sheets of music scattered over the ivory keys and most other surfaces were weighed down by stacked crime novels.

Lena listened to cats fighting in the laneway; their screeching drifted melodically beside the high pitched shrieks from Ben's shower pipes and was punctuated by the constant hum of mosquitoes passing closely by her earlobe. Ben turned the shower off and Lena heard a steady dripping sound which came from outside, at first believing it was someone urinating in the laneway, but then deciding it continued for too long for that to be true. She focused on the sound of Ben softly whistling in the bathroom next door and drifted to sleep.

An annoying clicking noise woke Lena; Ben was lighting a candle on the writing desk.

'The mosquitoes are huge', he whispered as he placed the cigarette lighter back down on the desk.

He waited for the candle to reach and liquefy its citronella wax, before removing the towel from around his waist and draping it over the wire chair. The room was dark but the flame from the candle was growing and bathed his silhouette. Ben crawled beside Lena, who was overwhelmed by the thick stench of mosquito deterrent which had now filled the room.

'This is so perfect,' Ben whispered, somewhat oblivious to Lena's discomfort.

She said nothing and put her arms around him, tracing her fingers over his back as he lay beside her. Lena paused her caressing when a sound was heard from elsewhere in the flat. A key was searching for a lock.

'Jules?' she queried.

'Don't worry, he won't come in here,' Ben assured.

Lena listened further as Ben's flatmate made enough noise to frighten off the cats in the laneway as he fumbled through the front door. 'Drunk,' she thought as she heard the same steady dripping noise as earlier, though this time the sound was nearer and lasted a shorter period. The bathroom door handle thumped hard against the plaster wall and she noticed the absence of a flushing noise, or a running tap. A television then turned on in another room, followed by the disconnected sounds of channel flicking; the irritating tune of which hovered over a familiar thud of light metal hitting and then spinning on the floor. Lena waited for the television audio to settle and then continued tracing her fingers over Ben's back.

The room was bright in the morning; it was overcast outside, but Ben had no curtain. The window was still open and the rubbish trucks were loud in the street. Glass bottles were being tipped into their trays and the stench of crushed rubbish was sifting up into his room.

Ben, dressed in beige trousers and a navy shirt, walked through the door and smiled at Lena. He had black, worn down shoes on and his face and manner was fresh.

'Hungry?' he shouted, over the sound of the rubbish trucks.

Lena sat up in Ben's bed; a repulsive feeling washed over her while she repeatedly rubbed her eyelids to rinse away the vision of dust particles which filtered through the bright light and appeared to suffocate the air. She squinted at Ben and his cheerful exuberance, croakily responding, 'Can I have a shower, Ben?'

'Of course, Jules won't be up for hours, just use my towel. I have to start at nine, so we should leave in twenty.'

There was no lock on the bathroom door and Lena felt uncomfortable being naked. The shower had a partially unhinged plastic curtain that wrapped and adhered to her body like cling wrap as she washed her hair. She looked at the hair infested soap which lay in the clogged dish attached to the tiled wall and thought of how disgusting Ben's flatmate was. With minimal amount of physical contact, Lena turned off the taps and stepped out of the tub, directly into her purposefully positioned thongs. She smelt warm toast as she dried herself with Ben's towel and twisted her hair into a bun high on her head.

Wearing her blue rolled up jeans and white singlet, Lena walked with Ben to the city centre where he worked.

The arcade was busy when they arrived.

'I'll meet you back here at two,' Lena said while she stood beside the entry to the bookstore where Ben hated to work. She then left the arcade to where the sun was shining and business people were flooding footpaths. She pushed her headphones in her ears and hurried out of the city which always felt hectic to her. Lena liked Sydney but it was different from anywhere she had ever lived. It was a city full of contradictions which both interested and numbed her.

By midday Lena was heading back into the city again, to meet Ben. She took the path through Hyde Park and sat on a bench to watch and contemplate all the people walking past. Mostly, they were trendy and if they weren't, then they were fashionably unfashionable. Many walked with an air of importance and a manner of arrogance; some shuffled with more of a mist than an air, but still with plenty of arrogance. She collected her things and kept walking, back to the arcade's entrance. Lena felt uncomfortable being amidst so many people and kept her headphones in her ears and avoided eye contact with passersby. Everyone hurried in pairs or groups and they carried opaque plastic bags from trendy boutiques, stopping regularly at windows and dissecting mannequins in store displays. It was all foreign territory to Lena, who hated shopping and didn't see the point in fashion or mainstream culture. She was a misfit in most ways and it seemed as though Sydney highlighted this, but could also complement it.

A tap on the shoulder and Lena turned to see Ben standing beside her. She took her headphones out and hugged him. Ben took Lena's hand. 'Let's get out of here'.

Ben and Lena stopped by a small food outlet in Kings Cross, where culture hungry mortals hummed outside. A woman with dangerous looking high heels stood beside the entrance, slowly smoking a cigarette. Inside, the bain-marie was glowing under heat lights and two men worked behind the counter where hot fat dripped from the top of a tier shelf ledge behind them, and splashed onto the earth-coloured encrusted perimeter of a deep fryer. A sign buzzed a neon green light on the adjacent end of the counter and below this flickering 'Fresh' symbol, were rows of metal trays that housed shreds of faded lettuce leaves and white speckled tomato quarters. Lena glanced over the contents and inhabitants of the shop, looking at their wan faces, the halogen and fluorescent lights above, and the dehydrated food. The only depth of colour to be found in this place was the dirt, which was everywhere and Lena stood, considering how it could exist at all, this grime pulsing hub of vitamin D deficiency. A man with grey skin appeared in front of Lena and grunted loudly as he gestured toward the salads that she was staring at. She jumped and quickly responded

'I'm still deciding'

Ben called out for hot chips as he walked back from the fridge with two small plastic bottles in his hand. Ben and Lena left the shop with their drinks and a paper bag full of hot chips. They passed by the dangerously heeled woman who was lighting another cigarette and followed the steps down to the wharf where they sat on the decking, below a ritzy waterside hotel, and ripped open the now transparent paper bag. Everything glittered in this alcove of wealth; the docked yachts were grand and gleaming, the surrounding apartment windows were clean, and the people sparkled from the triangular reflection which bounced between the water, the windows and their assortment of jewellery.

'Jules!' Ben was jumping and waving frantically. 'Jules!' he yelled out down towards the street.

Lena turned and looked down the pier to see a tall, hunched man walking with a bag over his shoulder.

'Jules!' Ben yelled louder.

The man stopped and looked irritably towards Ben who was swinging his arms, gesturing him to come. Lena stood up, sheltering her eyes from the afternoon suns glare with her hand, and she tried to focus on the figure in the distance, but could decipher only a hint. 'Thin, dark hair, petulant,' she thought.

Ben raised the empty chip bag with hopeful lure to the man, who responded with a careless flick of his hand before continuing his lurch and disappearing up the steps to the gardens.

Ben reached for the empty drink bottles, 'Well, that's Jules anyway, we'll catch up with him later,' he said defensively.

'What does he do? Where's he going?' Lena questioned.

'He's just doing his thing,' Ben snapped as he turned toward the flow of people who were now arriving. 'Let's head home'.

'But does he work?' Lena pressed.

'Yeah, he works for the council. Picks up rubbish, cuts back trees and whatnot.' Ben was clearly irritated by his friend. 'He goes to the pub a bit too. I think they're actually paying him to be there now!' His voice was smug. 'You know, wash glasses, dry glasses, fill glasses and whatever.'

Ben's bad mood stopped Lena from asking more questions about his flatmate, but she continued to think about him.

The door to Ben's flat was open when they arrived. Ben went inside first and looked for signs of anything missing. There was clothing over the floor in the living room and the television was on. The windows were open and empty beer bottles rolled in the breeze on the ground beneath a sofa, where a broken ceramic plate rested upon with silver coins scattered inside. Nothing had changed.

'He's a moron!' Ben shouted.

Lena closed the front door and nibbed the lock behind her. The door to Jules bedroom was open and Lena slowed to look inside. It was a smaller room than Ben's and it had no window. There was a mattress on the floor with a blanket scrunched up in the centre and a black backpack with wires hanging out in the corner. A poster of a woman with dark hair and red lips was taped crooked and low down on the wall. The woman wore a gold bikini and stood in an unnatural position with her hip cocked.

Ben called out from the kitchen. 'Lena, check this out!'

Lena put her bag down next the sofa, beside a cockroach dead on its back. She walked into the kitchen and found Ben standing on the sink looking out the narrow window. He tapped the bench. 'Hop up!'

Lena jumped up and looked out the window. She saw a man in the neighbouring building dressed in a smart outfit and holding a champagne glass. He was posing in front of a camera on a tripod and periodically smiling toward it. He appeared to be alone. The lights were dim and the curtains were mostly drawn. A table covered with alcohol stood behind him. He leaned against the table and looked seductively towards the camera lens. The flash went off and he resumed a miserable appearance. A moment later he did it again. This time he messed up his hair with his hands and undid the top two buttons of his shirt. He lounged on the table and raised his glass. He looked away from the camera and his mouth was moving. He was laughing and smiling and seemed to be talking. The flash went off again and then his mouth stopped moving. The corners of it fell downwards. The corners of his eyes were pulled down with it.

'Can you see anyone else there?' Ben asked.

'No,' Lena replied.

The man took one more photograph and then moved to a computer which stood behind the tripod. Lena moved the dirty dishes which were piled on of the sink and claimed their position with her knees. She could see the man's computer screen now.

'He's uploading the photos,' she said to Ben, who was now standing inside the fridge door and looking dismally at the block of cheese and beer that it contained. The man stood up and walked to the window, aggressively opening the curtains. Lena jumped down. She felt ashamed for watching him. She felt sorry for him, too.

'I think he saw me, Ben.'

'Don't worry,' Ben replied. 'People always get caught watching each other. You'll get used to it.'

Lena had only ever lived on the ground in weatherboard houses in her home town which was rural and private, where people only saw one another when they went out. She was both excited and nervous about moving to an apartment in a big city.

'Shall we go and look at places tomorrow, Ben? We only have two days left.'

'I don't start work 'til three, so we could look first thing.'

'What time will you finish?'

'Nine. It's late night shopping in the arcade.'

Lena leant into Ben. She felt worried about everything; about leaving Ben for another two months while she went home to organise her move, and about finding a secure apartment and job. And she worried about Ben's flatmate, Jules.

'I don't want to go home, Ben,' she said as she pressed herself closer to him.

'I don't want you to go either.' Ben stopped himself from continuing, 'Let's go out.'

They walked along the steep streets around Ben's home and up to the junction. The sun was sinking and the characters walking alongside them began to filter to an alternate state, in harmony with the light sifting away. Trendy people were trotting into doorways in groups and the lonely ones were heading outside. It was Thursday night and Sydney was ready for the weekend already. Cars were fluent in both directions on Darlinghurst Road and horns rang out incessantly. Ben ordered Pizza while Lena sat on a step outside and watched the street and she began to feel more confident in her abilities to adapt to Ben's city. They walked down to the pier again with their pizza and beer and sat under the warm night sky. Lena felt the alcohol invigorate her personality almost immediately, she was on a high from anticipation and she adored how totally anonymous she felt in Ben's city. Everyone seemed important and busy and this rendered her insignificant which she took great comfort in. She opened another drink and lay back on the deck with her head resting on Bens shoulder.

Mozart rang out from Lena's mobile at 7am the following morning. Ben found his numb arm sandwiched between Lena's stomach and his mattress. He pulled it from underneath her and swung it to the alarm. The music stopped. Seven minutes later, Mozart played again. Lena was face down in the middle of the pillow, she groaned and moved her head to give one eye vision.

'Shall we?' Ben asked.

'No,' she replied.

'Come on let's find somewhere to live, Lena.'

Lena slowed, on her way out of the apartment, by Julian's door which was slightly open. She could see a body lying spread out over the mattress; it was entirely unconscious, unwashed and heavy. She looked away and caught up to Ben who was waiting beside the elevator in the hallway.

Ben and Lena sat in a café and sifted through pages of lease listings. They visited dozens of apartments and made a shortlist which attempted to accommodate Lena's need of somewhere light enough to keep plants alive. The list was eventually narrowed down to two flats near the city centre, both had small, west facing windows; murderous to any foliage, yet affordable.

'I'll meet you back here at nine.' said Lena as she took the small bunch of keys from Ben's hand. 'It's the green one, right?'

Ben nodded and Lena put the keys in her pocket and walked in the direction of Ben's flat.

Lena pushed one half of the double doors open and walked up seven flights of stairs, she held the green key in her hand until she reached the front door of Ben's flat, which she found open again. Lena put the keys back in her pocket and nudged the creaking door. A man stood in the middle of the room. He was tall, broad and thin; his hair was dark and his clothing dirty. The man's eyes lifted and ceased upon Lena, injecting an intense stare. It was not quite four o'clock and he was holding a beer from out of the fridge and the block of cheese was on the table. She thought how disgusting he was as she introduced herself.

'I'm Lena. You must be Julian.'

His gaze remained fixed on her and didn't shift or blink as he began to smile. His shoulders fell slightly and his back straightened more as he chuckled and took a swig from his bottle, making an obnoxious noise after he swallowed. He laughed some more and raised the glass bottle toward Lena.

'Hi Lena,' he said, with a voice scratched and rough, but wet with alcohol.

'Ben gave me his key while he's at work. I won't stay,' she explained as he took a step closer to her.

Lena looked to the ground and walked past him, down the hallway and into the bathroom. She closed the door behind her and stared in the mirror as she listened carefully. She heard no steps but the floorboards creaked in the hallway and the narrow band of light between the door and floor made a sudden shift to darkness. Lena felt her face burn and her instincts reprimand her as she remembered that there was no lock on the bathroom door. She turned the sink taps on aggressively and the pipes shrieked. The noise seemed to help drown out her thoughts. The door handle shuddered as it was caressed from the other side and while water splashed on the mirror, the door handle began to slowly rotate clockwise until the sound of Mozart reverberated off the bathroom tiles, and Lena snatched her phone from her pocket. She answered the phone and kept her eyes fixed on the door's wooden handle, which paused when she spoke. 'Ben?'

The handle then began to reverse, turning anti-clockwise until it reached its origin.

'Hi, Beautiful.' Ben yelled over crowds in the arcade.

Lena watched light filter under the doorway again, in harmony with the sounds of creaking wood panels.

'It's crazy here.' Ben continued.

'Here too.' Lena whispered.

'Sorry it's a mess.'

'No. Not that.'

'Oh. Is Jules home?'

'Yes.'

'He should be at work?'

'He's not.'

'I have to go Lena, it's busy and loud here. I'll see you at nine."

Ben hung up before Lena could say more. She stood in the bathroom and frantically typed a message on her phone to him: 'Call Julian, distract him. He's drunk and I need to get out.'

Lena watched the light under the door and listened hard, while she waited for Ben's reply, which never came. Struggling to hear past the sound of her heart beating, she turned the sink taps on stronger, hoping to drown out that pulsating beat; her knuckles turning white from the pressure. She swallowed, quietly, before slowly opening the door to the hallway. Lena slid through the gap, her senses alert as she crept along the edge of the hallway with her back softly rubbing the wall. Floorboards weakened beneath her feet and seemed to whimper with each gentle step as they led her to the open lounge space where she could see her exit door. The door was now closed and the lock clicked in. The air was still and she could see no one, but the cockroach on its back. Lena paused; she could hear only the water still splashing in the bathroom sink, her palms were sweating, and then Mozart rang loud. She snatched the phone from her pocket.

'Ben?' she said.

'Lena, get out!' Ben's voice was trembling, 'get out now!' He yelled.

Lena stepped closer toward the door and she listened through the phone to Ben's shoes hitting the pavement. The move brought sight of Julian, who was leaning casually against the doorframe to his bedroom with bare feet, a smile still on his face and a bottle still in his hand. Lena stopped and stood still as Julian raised his bottle, bowing his head in unison with his lifting elbow. He moved slowly and his smile fell away as his head rose and his dark, glassy eyes fixed on hers once more. Lena pressed the phone harder to her ear, in an effort to shift the weight of her senses, from vision to sound. She listened carefully to Ben's running and she wondered why he was running. She listened to the rhythm, distracting herself from her physical presence, concentrating hard on that rhythm. She heard noises, thumping and slapping noises, sounds against pavement and her mind saw Ben's black soled shoes scuffing as she envisioned them hitting the concrete. He was running so hard, so fast, so frantically. Lena imagined the shins above those black soles weakening and Ben's knee bones aching with each hit to the floor. She held Julian's gaze; an intimidating stare, as she pressed the phone closer to her lips.

'I don't think I can, Ben,' she whispered.

Lena listened harder to Ben's gallop sounding through the phone. She heard him gasping for breath, and his throat sounded rough as it searched for air. She tried to merge her mind's focus with Ben's running rhythm, calculating the distance he was covering, while Julian shuffled from his doorway. He moved wearily, though it was clear to Lena that this was only a preliminary tired, a look that appeared to be collecting his drunken body, one weighted limb after the other, unifying them and drawing strength, gaining focus and steadying himself until he was standing strong and threatening. He walked toward Lena, who remained still. She continued to focus on the pulsating rhythm that echoed through the phone and the more she concentrated, the more it became clear what she was hearing. The sounds were multiplied; the pavement was being hit twice at the same speed.

Julian stood tall in front of Lena, and reached out to touch her. Lena lost her focus with the sound of Ben's voice.

'Lena,' he said. 'Julian's with me.'

Ian C. Smith

Two Figures on a Bed

She would thank him after sex
disconcerting him considering
her impression of an effigy
immediately preceding this gratitude.
He yearned for remembered arousal
kept his life a secret from her
yet expected her to know what he desired.

He knew she wanted him for herself
so her lack of sexiness puzzled
threw him off his predatory trail.
She praised him, bought gifts
while he craved chiaroscuro, theatre
a rough, brilliant darkness, a tension
missing in her scholarly demeanour.

She had been annihilated by the end
believing her luck with men doomed
feels she deserves to be a caring wife
chiding her fear of sexual boldness.
Tracking coolly through his past bedrooms
he thinks he should have spanked her
used her in drunken porn flick athletics.

Jim Davis

The Bard

Let me look at you.
In need of a shave,
Hair carefully combed,
High forehead shining,
And yet…
That too, too solid flesh
Has melted as into a dew,
And left — what?
A name? An enigma?
Do they know your father
Was once fined
For leaving an unauthorized dung heap
On Henley Street?
Think of the neighbors!
Very English somehow.
But Dad didn't deliver on security.
Off to London.
Acting no less.
'The Shakespeare lad
Has fallen in with bad company.'
Yet he rose.
Too right.
He rose by writing
One damned scribble after another.
The pressure of production
Kept him at his desk
But he reclaimed the family name;
Went to London to see the Queen.
So when his writing days were long in shadow
He played the gentleman at ease.
And the plays and poesy?
'Oh those?

'Prithee, do not concern me thus.
'They have had their use.
'Use them as you will.
'Many joyful days and bawdy souls;
'Grind them all to dust.
'I am done with all.
'What lamentable conceit
'To think they will
'Range beyond my orbit.'

Petri Ivalo Sinda

Meltdown Express

Through Lowdark and Poison Waterhole Creek we tear along past a massive white billboard scaled to peak hour highway attention spans — *Do Not Tap Accelerator In Time To Music* — before our 4K slog suddenly accordions from a flat-horizon three day sprint to a three hour needle eye crawl. This particular needle eye is an outer suburban corridor leading into the city nucleus proper, but even this far out it's packed tight with cars, street signs, protruding shop awnings, peek-a-boo traffic islands and wayward pedestrians versed in polyglot blasphemy. Just crawling with people. Riding shotgun, I try picturing the pedestrians as kangaroos: had I the wheel I'd be tempted to play Bumper Car.

Failing that, Grand Theft Auto IV.

'Check out the zombie limo,' Shane sneers, nudging his chin towards some car poolers visibly sick of each others' company. Shee-it. We've jammed up against the start of peak hour. Dead in the water. 'Folks,' Shane continues, 'we've had the special luck to end up smack bang in a mobile cemetery. Only it ain't too mobile just at this particular juncture.' His voice cracks with a little Marlene Dietrich: 'Break out ze colouring in books, boys… 'I reel away. My brain can't compute that voice coming out of a hyper muscled six foot and change Olympic rowing contender with bushy black hair and a jaw chiselled off Mt Olympus itself. Normally soft spoken and easygoing, he can't do a thing about his physical intensity.

Now that we're stalled, humidity begins to colonize my armpits. Lolling my head around in abstract disgust, I briefly catch a reflection of bloodshot eyes in the left wing mirror. Great. Slumping down and away from this sight, I let go and drift in free association, an anti-stress technique nabbed from my days with the cyber shamans. It strikes me that the cars all round us are cyborgs of one sort or another. Not just fuel injected bogan chariots but methamphetamine stoked too. A Francis Bacon marriage of meat and machine. Nothing alchemical though, just the mandatory urban sorcery of drugs and brake horsepower.

A sudden braying of *c'mon-get-going* car horns. I crane my head up just as the whole scrapmetal jungle heaves into motion again. My head snaps forwards, back, forwards. Thanks, Shane.

Massaging my neck, I distract myself from these new hurts by musing how the human halves of these automotive cyborgs only need to be as careless and tough hearted as the local conditions call them to be. The monstrous city up ahead is, I can tell, a place that's never known sentimentality. Already the streets look dirtier and more rundown than I would've thought imaginable for a world class western city. A burst city. In a sudden access of contempt I turn to Shane: 'Gun it already, *go go go!*' I shove his shoulder but he's already got the fear. His eyes are zipping back and forth trying to track fifty incoming vectors at once. A city of five million is simply too dense with incident after the balmy sensory deprivation of the desert nothingness. But Shane's good; a regular Neal Cassady. He gets on top of it. We make ground in little fits and starts. Our car squeezes a high-tension bow wave of desert time ahead of us, a tilted meniscus of adrenaline fought to a standstill that we can now just calmly exhale in mescaline skid and drift, displacing the empirical city. See, we have our drugs too, but they haven't helped our indolent trans-desert metabolisms handshake the supercharged city metabolism. Sweating it out in the Ford Durango, we're still becalmed in an ontological decompression chamber waiting to cycle us through to the new street reality awaiting us in Newtown.

Then Shane pokes his head out the window and yells *'Get out th' way ya arse clowns!'* I hide my face in my hands.

Motion returns. The wheels chew up the tarmac. We *growl* along. Irritated by the road's grittiness, the engine block stutters, an inhuman vibration that jack knifes our vertebrae at thirty hertz or something. Ignore it. I throw to the crowd, locking eyes with some backstreet kids treating their faces as billboards, spray painted graffiti eyes saying nothing, giving nothing away. Every Sydneysider's behaving as if they're spot lit on camera and being fêted the stardom owed them as birthright, heroes of their own little dramas welcome to ham it up for all they're worth. Lots of squabbling hand signals. Idle chaff of accents and dialects tossed back and forth. Muscular speech riding roughshod over those with a quaint penchant for good manners. Half overheard conversations parodying themselves. *Und so weiter.* Well, I'd been warned to expect an irreversible fast pace to sweep me away if I didn't learn to step onto curbs already running. And the sidewalks are no different than the roads, really; foot traffic dense as glaciers running fifty times fast forward, no give and take in sight. Now that's avalanche momentum.

'Cars sure do hold the reins here.' Malcolm offers up from the back seat. I just nod. Yeah, they're bolting along like so many wild stallions penned together too long. Unbridled liberation of energy. No brake on the chrome overspill. I love it.

Love it. The dirt, the noise, vulgarity, claustrophobia; the blinding window displays, the straggly repetition of the shops with yet more graffiti storming their barricades; the *Hellraiser* scaffolding retrofitted to building façades like humungous body piercing dioramas; the traffic helicopters, the flailing sirens of stranded ambulances hemmed in by bored and uncaring couriers; the capering antics of homeopathic street ninjas, the tinderbox winos who spent the night soaking in motor oil sumps, the gladdening sight of free range mascots in bear costumes, not to mention *al fresco* bizness execs toasting their egos by sprinting food down their gobs — god help me I'm loving it all. It's giving me a horn. Outside of sex my heart hasn't beat this fast in ages. The glorification of Rush. Sydney's patron saint is speed; automotive and chemical both. Cars racing; chromium bullet expresses that trounce all pedestrian rights. 'Beat it ya dickless wonders! I'm driving here, I'm driving here!' An ego-soaked city populated by cars, even more so than my ole home town. And yet here I am, dreaming I've forsaken Car City in pursuit of Culture, only to find more and faster cars.

While loving it.

'Man, the way they drive here,' Shane remarks, 'I can't believe more of 'em don't end up dead'f self inflicted natural causes.'

Malcolm agrees. 'It could be a high-collision sport!' he says, rubbing his hands. 'We should stitch up the television rights.'

'C'moffit, they're *slow*-pokes!' I object, but they know I'm only donning my Captain Contrary cape. I watch a car up ahead barrel through a red light stop. In Sydney an amber light evidently means 'Speed Faster *Now*.'

I sense we're past the main bottleneck. Movement comes more frequently now, lasts longer. The noise is intense.

We're all feeding on the excitement, though somewhat shamefacedly, it has to be said. It's tainted love after all.

A love for the toxic golden exhaust baking in this afternoon traffic and heat. Love for the hustling moves drivers pull as they zip together a wondrous labyrinth of kinetic energy — an energy that surges through the hubs and intersections, lurching along whenever there's a spare millisecond gap or someone's patience breaks and they go for it anyway. On the car stereo Bowie's wailing 'putting out the fire with the gasoline.'

'Can we stop for kebabs?' Mal complains. 'No!' we yell back. I'm reminded of the patrol boat in *Apocalypse Now*. Never get out of the vehicle. Always stay in the vehicle.

As the afternoon steeps towards dusk, the consensual hallucination of all this gridlock begins to suture together an ever more elaborate optical sculpture of zigzagging head lights and tail lights. The crazy wiring diagram of inner urban humanity, its semiotics too embrangled for decryption. I try rinsing my eyes with gentle fingertip rubs.

We are here at The Hub, Newtown, where half a dozen streets intersect. Northbridge, cubed. We are here at The Triangle, where three great massive pubs converge. And there's a train-line just below King Street as well. King Street to City Road, solid kilometres of shops marching single file either side of the road. Multi storey secondhand bookshops. Multi nation eateries. Tattoo parlours by the bushel. And we're also in the flight path of the airport, which, every few minutes, makes certain we don't forget it.

The 747s resemble lead blimps with chrome boomerangs for ailerons. They're so sluggish their shadows cast a pall of fear over Newtown. Well, over me anyway. They appear to only just clear the taller buildings when they taxi in for landing, scoring the sky with the violence of their passage. Bouncing and rebounding off the buildings all round, the metallic engine roar envelopes us, temporarily inhabits us, re tuning our spine antennae to inhuman frequencies, shrill machine dreams. I'm not especially fond of machines playing out their desires within me, looking for easy kicks. But then, looking all round, I don't really think I'm going to get much of a choice. Everything in sight is picking up the jet engine transmissions. Echoes spall off every which way, scattering off yet more surfaces, turning practically everything around into vibrating reeds...the whole shimmering field of iron, glass and steel erected around us is threatening to turn musical.

Does this stop me extending my senses, straining outwardly, hoping to kiss the sky?

Not one bit.

I'd *like* the city to commune with me. Sing to me, if it feels so inclined. I tremble, expectant, hopeful of success. After all, there's no denying my infatuation for the energy, for the sheer scale of it all. Everything Ye Olde Hometown couldn't cough up.

I crane my head up and search about, waiting for the towers to burst into music. I even wind down the window and stick my head out. Ugh — I forgot the air's monoxide heavy here. Blow like a shotgun butt to the lungs. I'm coughing ozone soot, while Sydney's mouldering beneath leaden air.

'Hey quit it!' Shane is sore at me not for coughing loudly but because I'm still gawking around like a kid. Embarrassing.

Well…I have reason enough. It's called excitement. Everything's more vertical here. The terrain close to the harbour is heaped. Crenellated bays mount up into clumped hills so that rich people can pile the skyscrapers on thick. And there you have it, simple as that. Endless visual drama. Even the trains are double storey. Somewhere above, up there, jetliners stretch the city to new dimensions by luring our highways off into the sky, where they long to merge with the ceaseless highways of the atmospheric jetstream.

I notice only then that I've been grooving in my seat to some vintage 12" remix of 'Living on the Ceiling.' Infectious, nicht Wahr? Musicians are subliminal terrorists.

And yet, and yet…the central business district does not sing. True, it barks out noise, sure enough, the usual idiot glossolalia of car horns, DON'T WALK claxons, reversing streetsweepers, buses braking, people swearing, laughing, ordering beer…but no, no, this apeshit symphony does not bring its instruments together in soul communion.

'What micro climate is this?' Malcolm whinges, jarring me out of my electric reverie. He sounds like a fugitive from another time zone. Which, after three days inside a car, I suppose he is. 'I mean,' he continues, 'how're we expected to adapt to…*this*?'

Trying not to be irritated by his naïveté, I put him at his ease. 'Aw, don't sweat it! I'm sure they got vendors with off the shelf psychopathologies. Kooky pills for all occasions, all yer socialising needs catered to — one sickness fits all!'

It's not Malcolm's answering look of contempt that makes my face burn — it's his air of superiority. He tilts his head to the side like Margaret Thatcher and moues, 'Did you discover your yuppie setting or something?'

I glare back. It's become clear Mal wants to hoof it to Melbourne instead. I try appeasing him. 'C'mon man, welcome to the League of

Slightly Ordinary Beings. Or, as we like to call it, the Human Race.' I sweep out my arms, taking in all the pedestrians.

'Age before beauty, then,' he counters. 'You go right ahead and fit yourself up a straitjacket — don't forget to drop us a postcard.'

He's no use when he's in this mood. Me neither. I seek out the city centre, approaching faster now as the gridlock eases more and more and cars peel off down side streets like liberated blood cells. Ouch. I turn too quick. My head swims. Haven't eaten today. Hyperglycaemic crash on the way. Meh.

There's a queer moment as a feeling of vertigo suddenly flashes over into apotheosis. But this is not a vertigo founded in height — it's founded in the free space above, the whole wide sky, and the light, the opalescent light. And the vertigo's not out there. It's in me. Whoa. Moments of such intensity catch fire. My head has to stretch to accommodate new dimensions — I can feel my skull readjusting its suture lines, giving itself more latitude to extend and build some more extra rooms upstairs (I could do with a penthouse suite, but I have a gut feeling I'll end up with a grubby cubbyhole).

I think I know what this inner vertigo's about. It's *the scale* of the city that's trying to sing to me. The impact of scale I felt as a kid when first in Sydney. The first time I claimed the word 'metropolis.' Transformative.

It's only as a kid that anything really affects you, changes you. Once adult, we only tweak. As a kid (when adults are twice your size and stride the continent as giants), you're allowed to blow your mind with *scale*. It's a big, world expanding feeling: visits to huge cities no longer prove frightful. They're transfigurative instead. You end up recalibrating your head to a bigger world, a bigger sense of life, and become determined to live bigger, bolder. That's when you truly find out the size of the world and your size relative to it. Your place.

Bullshit, clearly. Kids worship winning. Kids over-dramatize everything because they've got something lavish called 'imagination.' As we age we shed the glorious but false magnitudes of the world in favour of clearer, tinier doses of reality. We want to sort ourselves out, live up to responsibilities not fantasies. That generally means accepting a different place. There's only room for three podium winners.

Really though, at heart, we'd settle for just being able to cope. To function is enough, just…good enough.

…except that ends up being pretty much *all* we can achieve, because everything about a city is orders of magnitude bigger than human imagination. A city processes us through its monster guts, mills us into shape, sends us on our way. Could a cave man have dreamt up Rome? Could even a literate Sumerian have imagined New York?

Shane catches me searching up and down Parramatta Road. He thinks I'm sneering at a broken down car up ahead but my head is too busy throbbing. He points, says: 'I think that tyre's finally discovered its receding hairline!' Then he frowns and asks why I didn't laugh along.

I'm not even as big as that side street. I have no right to point to the Blue Mountains and shout 'I'm as good as those damn mountains!'

The trick is to not flinch. To not shrink any further.

Paralysis seems a decent option.

Good enough … to function is good enough. Yeah, that'd be mintox. Sure. But I wasn't born with an encyclical in my hands decreeing I need to be as good as the Andes. Hell, I'm not even as good as the Darling Range.

Not even the tyre dump at the local tip.

'Wanna pull over?' Shane demands. I shake my head, don't reply. That's because I'm grinding my teeth. They've locked up again. I'll have to loosen them up, work this sick vertigo out of myself. Do the spiritual regurgitation act. Yeah, it's gone sick. It's turned bad. Something's building in me, and it isn't car sickness. At least not the usual kind. What wazzat Henry Miller debut — *The Air conditioned Nightmare*? Yeah, that.

I should laugh. I *want* to; what's futile is to *avoid* quailing before this apotheosis. Quick. Try something — anything. Go further, hold onto the vertigo. Hold onto the aspect of it that recapitulates that first childhood encounter with *scale*, back on that first trip to Sydney. It's an unexpected gift, re experiencing the subjectivity of childhood — so bloody treat it as such! Artists strive after just this very thing after all. Matisse, Henri Rousseau, Paul Klee. All the usual suspects. They zero in on that mercurial life cusp of choosing dependence or freedom and re-inhabit it, reliving that whole critical phase of deciding whether one's whole life will be blanket acceptance or asking questions questions questions. Whether it's to be *joy* or *fear* at being ruled by the Platonic Reality of Received Ideas.

No wonder we root around so much for surrealist drugs to scramblefuck our systems.

Orwell's *1984* or Plato's regime of Ideal Forms of the Good. Really, which is worse? (Any great difference?)

We find our place by rebelling against our place. On some level people in the western world desire that forsaken childhood feeling of colliding headfirst with new realities — if only to see who's stronger! It's us against the mountains! Who's up for an arm wrestle? You, Ben Nevis? You, Kosciusko?

I could go a Mount Fuji about now.

Long relegated to instinct, I dredge up the old hard won recognition that, up to a certain age, identity loves to test itself against the limitations posed by interface with other identity systems, be they tribal or institutional. To find by rebelling. But now, with my head bumping against the seat rest in stop motion gridlock, neon advertising dissolving before my eyes into jewelled liquid calligraphy of seraphic quality, what I manage to appreciate now is that regardless of the choice made, whatever the practical outcome, the true gold is the feeling that spills out the side, the sense of expansiveness followed by the wonder of settling on a version of being you can claim as your own. Hey presto: self acceptance and a self *to* accept in the one tricked out Chrissie present. The grand unification of conviction and confidence.

...which we largely forget as we let the career machine lump us onto clearly defined promotion on-ramps and incremental pay-increase treadmills. All our sins remaindered.

'Okay. That's it. We need to get a beer into you.' Shane jerks the car to a stop. Trust him to notice. Simpler to give in. I nod curtly. Something unlocks in my jaw and I manage to squeak: 'Yep, here's good as anywhere.'

He's only a little concerned for me. Mostly he's pissed off I've funked out on him. Not the driving companion he signed up for. Aww great. Now I've fucked up for true. I rub my squirming chest. Something's building up in me alright. I keep thinking I've thought it all clear out, drained the 'inner vertigo' out of me, led it away, but it's still here, the thunderstorm weather still building inside me. I don't know what I'm feeling. It's awesome. It's huge. It's nameless.

That freaked me out, first time I heard a girl say she didn't know what she was feeling. *How can you not know what you're feeling, as you're feeling it? You're creatures* of *feeling!*

Maybe this is the same goddamn thing.

Malcolm notices me clutching my chest. I relax my grip and flick my shirt as if banishing imaginary lint. Better he think I'm obsessive compulsive than...than...what? What am I? *What's happening in me?*

It almost comes to me, but something shears aside with a desperate will —

Damn oh god damn. My flesh is fidgeting. I'm giving myself the creeps. Alcohol. Pot. Cyclobarbital. Alka Seltzer. Motion Lotion. Yes: time to pray to Bacchus! Yes. Gotta put a note of upandatem in my voice: 'Come on then! Let's sample the local, see if they make correct weight.'

'And kebabs!' Malcolm insists. We have to laugh. How can a stick figure put away so many calories?

Marvelling at the exorbitant parking fees posted up nearby, we stretch our legs as we scope out the chrome moon annealed to the lavender dusk. I savour how pollution must be the greatest imaginable boon to artists. Sydney harbour must really rock at about this time, when smog is at its sweetest. I hope it can give L.A. a run for its money.

We set sail for the nearest Chippendale bar. The cooling air freeze dries our sweat and refreshens our energy. We're all giddy for beer after four thousand Ks.

But Mal doesn't like the look of the yuppie bar. 'If I go in there I'll die of celebrity monoxide.' We examine the Glitterball Baroque inside. He's probably right but…

I try again: 'When will ya do me a favour and just be one with the people?'

'When you stop drunk dialling Santa Claus!'

Shane and I set off again, *tsk*ing at Mal.

But my head's swimming. Loping along, I can't help thinking back on that adult imperative to assume responsibilities; coping, functioning; and I think: groovy how we've managed to become functionaries of the human soul, stewards of a glory forever deferred to some future stage of human spiritual development. Meanwhile, punch in and earn the bread.

Imagination, after all, doesn't guarantee any victories. Imagination being also the source of the keenest tortures we ever bestow upon ourselves. As in when we use it to compare our almighty insignificance with our unlived, *potential* significance.

Our drive to defy futility has to be ruthless; steel willed. It's the gap in our expectations that burns. That kills. Fuels the nothingness we feel when we don't measure up to the destiny we'd allotted ourselves since childhood; since our parents made us feel we'd been given a papal directive to go live like Achilles, like Casanova, like Napoleon Dynamite.

Falling short the slowest death of all. Lose grip on the scale of your imagination and you shrink to a dot. It happens. Can't be helped. Most lives are false lives. Best just to mask it and carry on with a hey and a ho.

Shit, evolution must have invented imagination just to get us past adolescence alive. It's surplus from then on though, an apparition of the junk genes. Anyone afterwards who still lives by imagination cannot have fully matured. Is still juvenile. Unweaned. Enfeebled. This must be true. It burns a hole in my guts.

So what. I want to burn.

You're never too old to rebel against 'knowing your place', that ole slave morality.

Shane notices I'm not with them before I do. He stops, throws me a look. I look down. I've stopped in my tracks. Malcolm doubles back alongside, gives me his best Sherlock Holmes squint. 'Wassap with you, sunstroke?' His hands are raised, querying the air, wondering whether he's going to have to intercept me fainting away. I can't tell him anything. My jaw's locked again. Useless grinding. I just stand there, swaying like a mongoloid sunflower. Shane slaps his hands above his knees then jams them outwards in supplication. *C'mon already!* He turns and gesticulates like a stage magician at all the Tinnitus Deco inside the bar, waiting to rattle for us. He's pretty keen to get acquainted with the local brew. Trembling, I can only shake my head. Shane and Malcolm glance at each other. I have to say something.

This 'vertigo' I've been feeling, what is it really? Try look at it directly and it shears aside. But I've snuck a quick sideways look into my soul and — and —

It's the ache of self exile, the regret of willed self-alienation. It's fear of cutting off friends and family in my loosey goosey pursuit of the magic unknown, of the magic dice of unknown chances. A lottery of fanciful hopes, no doubt — after all, most often the winds of good fortune blow tumbleweeds. Oh really, the time to move Over East was ten years ago. A cleaner break then. Put down too many roots since. Will miss them all too much now. My head slips downwards, bounces on its neck springs. Wincing, I close my eyes. I'm not in my body, I'm considering the past. I'm trying to will myself back, reoccupy a feeling, a memory. But nothing tunes in. I'm adrift. I reopen my eyes, stare at the ground between my shoes. Driving all this way over here, I've just guaranteed myself my heart will cave in. Vertigo of certain loneliness. That's where I stand: on the brink of dead cert loneliness.

I haven't informed Mal I absolutely refuse to sharehouse with him. The only way to relocate is to go it alone.

Say something.

Three sharp practice breaths through the nose and I manage to unhinge my jaw.

'Guys,' I plead, 'let's instead find a park, kick the footy while it's still light.' Light…my memory of our desert drive has been replaced by a hypnagogic reel. My head pulses silver and chrome. I sure as shit gotta drain out this weird physical energy. Or I'll explode. Or something. It's the something that worries me. 'C'mon fellahs, one last time … '

'Aww get real. What light?'

'Okay, a small clearing then, under a streetlight. Let's celebrate with a hack.' My voice cracks. 'No stopping till we get a triple hack.' They don't even deign to reply, just turn on their heels and split the front doors wide open. And still I can't budge. I'm sick of knowing what I'm going to do next. I feel invisible corridors hemming me in; joined cages in the exact shape of my bodily silhouette as I carve my own path through space time. My own small, private path of minimum choices, any larger life forbidden me.

Fuck *that*. I picture myself pushing head and shoulders through these self bored corridor walls, searching everywhere beyond for the new life, the secret life; that life which is always elsewhere. I want to break out of the script. I want to live big. I'm not too old. *That's why I came here!*

But no, oh no. I'm comparing again, revisiting the terror of potentiality. That's why I'm paralyzed! I'm having clairvoyant shots of futures I won't set foot on. Just like every other stupid jerk, I've fallen for it too! Agonizing lacks, chances not grabbed…futile comparisons…aw man, too stupid for words.

Shit's sake. Talk about stuck. Talk about hopeless.

I wish they'd look back at me. I'd spill. I'd fess everything. I'd apologize for coming with them on this trip.

No. What I really want to do is to melt myself down and reform again brand new, blank as an egg. I wish I could reopen myself to those post-schooling realities I'd pre experienced before I'd even gotten to them. It's what artists do, after all. They want everything fresh. The cobwebs cleared. *More than anything I want to look forward to something.*

And…if I loosened scale once, as a kid…I must be able to do it again?

Hope bursts throughout me. A prickly warmth that elevates me from inside. At last. At last!

So then, transfixed by this hope for some all-destroying inner disaster to wipe me out, cancel me back to embryo innocence, I find myself imaging any number of different ways to *be*, mental images like illustrated playing cards spraying past my face, doorways of light and hope and chance. My neck arches involuntarily and I find I'm up on tiptoes, straining for a new light as my mouth gapes open searching for ecstasy, my tongue questing about just as it does in the full straining outreach of orgasm. And it's here. The ecstasy of innocence is here for me, answering me. Sweet pure deliverance. Wowee. This feeling spears me and I hang there simply vibrating at the end of it, glowing inside in companionable likeness to Bernini's St. Teresa.

The sweet wonderful thing about ecstasy is how it grants absolute total forgetting of past and future. My eyes flutter open long enough to catch on the nearby skyscrapers just beyond Ultimo and Haymarket. Then I kind of go out like a light. All this apotheosis of imagination just collapses like a deck of cards. It's like my eyes fail me. *But yet, for this precious instant, my futures have become open to me:*

Soon enough I'll discover Sydney is chump change compared to Hong Kong. It is Sydney, cubed. And Hong Kong will prove to be just a suburb of Bangkok, ten million strong. And what of the mountainous towerpiles of New York, or the hapless clustering in Tokyo and Mexico City?

I rummage among my futures, chasing after each one but they're like a flight of starlings exploding out of a tree. I grab at them. I want to catch history in my hands and hold on for all I'm worth.

I watch Earth's cities extend urban corridors until they join together into one global synaptic entity, forming a crisscrossing cosmopolis, suburbs beyond the horizons…I can make out shoulder to shoulder high rises bathing in celestial smog, only the pinprick radiance of their lighted windows piercing the prevailing thick red ambience (colour it Pantone Entropy)…on clearer days asphalt skies colonize the windows…no surprise that the towerblocks will become great big capacitors of solitude, tenants neurotically hoarding the diminishing virtues still open to the human spirit…bonsai skyscrapers for a belittled people nesting in cranial penthouses of virtual reality… monogrammed ruins the future will never decrypt…for a while you'll still be able to mortgage your way into those celestial pyramids hauling their ferroconcrete tonnage above all this ruddy heat haze… cities astride pylons, postmodern Stonehenges on an Olympian scale…

but I come to a point where I observe the Earth almost entirely paved over, elephantiasis of the concrete. No more room. Time to build up. Well, there's always low Earth orbit. Fill it with skyscrapers already. *Neutronium dense public housing. Suburbs beyond event horizon.*

And there I'll be, in between somewhere. Always leaving home. City hopping on the exile express, my days lived out spinning gravel underfoot. The abstract conquests of sightseeing will just have to replace friends, I guess. I'll have to find happiness among the family of roads.

The funny thing? …I don't feel too bad about it. It's not unnatural to bury the Earth in concrete. After all, *every*thing that is to come remains the work of man in the end. It's easy to see this once you consider cities as nothing but the latest extensions of our bodies; a new kind of epidermis, that's all. We're symbionts, us city folk. Giants astride continents astride oceans. Gods of variable scale. At last I'm free to shout 'We're…*nearly* as good as those damn mountains!'

In other words Sydney is going to work out for me just fine. *Gotta Say Yes to Another Excess.*

I open my eyes properly, blink away the Polaroids from the future.

'Save me a schooner!' I cry out, trying to skip after Shane and Mal but only tangling myself up in my legs. The stiffness hasn't quite left me. I pause, work my jaw around. Hmm. That'll need a spot of Scotch and Dry lubricant. First I loosen my body with a li'l shake of the Elvis and throw off the evil vibes. A couple of ladies wolf whistle as if I've arrived to give their table a special performance. Play your cards right, Ladies…

I catch up to Shane and Mal; slaps on the back with High Fives for exclamation marks. Odd — this whole breakthrough epiphany thing is thanks to a wee little jaunt along the desert highway, of which all I remember now is luminous chrome streaking past in blinding rays that slit the retina.

Teri Louise Kelly

Autodidactic Masturbatory Addict

I.

It weren't hard to learn
even without an Idiot's Guide
like, there were only two choices
push or pull
practice makes perfect
perfection is a visible notion
come on over & do the twist
pick out the seeds
the blind lead the blind
into seminal brutality.

II.

I came upstairs
not literally…
expecting Leonardo Dicaprio
to be frozen inside someone else's dream
find her spread on the bed like hot rubber
dough nutting in shimmy black
satin bows & easy on/off platforms
i had the urge to don oilskin
slippery when wet
instead i bit her
& she bled out for me
as I kneaded her needs
satisfied mine
to Leonardo Dicaprio's appreciative smile.

III.

A water melon is not a sex toy
water melons have rights, I guess
but not fists,
fists have no rights,
fingers, maybe…
tongues, certainly,
the human frame
is dotted with orifices,
pin the tail on the donkey
join the dots, idiot…
that was how I failed in grade.

IV.

I watched her watching her own undercarriage
in the mirror,
as she mounted the stairs
turning herself on to narcissism
dreaming reptilian dreams
not starring Leonardo Dicaprio…
i followed the snail trail
to wonderland
& therein we built our own time;
razed ancient myths
fled into embryonic fluid
ate water melon with sticky fingers.

Benito Di Fonzo

Inappropriate Email to a Girl in Melbourne
(for Molly Stone)

Next Monday when you're on the Mascot Line I want you to get off at Redfern, and this time stay the night.

I'll kiss your eyelids open at dawn and convince you to chuck a sickie.

I'll coffee your torso under the covers with hot cuppings of caresses.

I'll remove the toasty doona and keep you amueslied.

I'll warm you with abysmal puns and fleecy neologisms till you chortle off the codeine karma of absinthe and the peppery merlot that you love so.

Then I'll breakfast upon your Ouroboros until you dictate a pantheon of deities over the station announcements succumbing from across the road.

Intermittently we'll rest with a little passive smirking.

And before we know it night will have fallen, and we'll order in, and slowly reveal our sauces.

Till finally we collapse to the sound of our labours echoed in the back lane by stray cats (and other rockabillies).

And the currawongs will guffaw at the garbage men, and it will be dawn again.

But let's face it, I'll probably stink by then. And you'll probably want to go home.

It's just a suggestion.

See you Monday.

Á. N. Dvořák

Surbiton

You could see it even now.
The way he'd cut the filter's tip
With scissors from the jar.
His private smirks as it'd flip
And somersault away.
You'd catch his teeth
In movements quick;
The tiny jerks and flinches.
The thirsty pint,
The waiting Age.
His parching, sinewed skin.
You'd watch them wind him,
Even still,
The day's hard wearies won.
And then at night,
Could hear his jaws
That worked, and sawed, and splintered.
That sound
That hacked you
At your spine
And turned your mouth to cotton.
You'd have to up.
And to the sink
Above his littered plate;
Of bitten steak and stiff red chips.
To stand yourself a drink.
And then, but then:
You'd hear it.
The fox's screaming banshee cry
That cold that cuts the quick,
That curdles from inside.
She'd call you out to speak about:

Á. N. DVORÁK

The Hells.
You'd listen.
Then put down your glass,
Pad back to bed,
Always knowing. Knowing nothing,
And stare.
At that: Poor, sleeping spider
Flat back, raised legs and arms.
As he'd grind and gnaw
At nowt, and all
And that, which snuck,
And stayed.
Somewhere, underneath his gums.

Nathan Hondros

The Embrace

When she was sure she was alone, Mathilde waded into the bay until the tepid water was up to her waist and closed her eyes. She thought of her mother coming down the stairs, in a blue silk dressing gown, backlit by silver light; it was as if she could really see her. But what now? Sometimes, when she made up these stories, she thought of herself chest deep in water, as she was then, swirling it around her with stretched out palms. She tried it a little. Mother would stop on the stairs and say, '*Look. My little girl can swim.*' Although she couldn't. She stayed in the water, moving it around her, making up stories about her mother until she heard the bell on the gate. She turned towards the shore and saw her uncle in the distance, his head down, walking quickly between the garden and the house. He didn't see her. A briefcase swung from his arm and his hat was fixed tight on his head, screwed down like a nut on a bolt; he didn't even take it off when he went through the kitchen door.

Mathilde could see Maxine, the housekeeper, in the kitchen window, startled as the man bustled through. From where she was standing in the water, Mathilde could see most of the house. The window behind which her mother lay in bed was hidden by the leaves of the plane tree, like pairs of open hands, draping and obscuring. Maxine spoke to the uncle, although the girl couldn't hear a word. *Mother's eyes open. She can hear him speaking, from her room, because he is always shouting at Maxine.* For a moment, she stopped moving in the water and reminded herself that her mother hadn't opened her eyes, not properly, for months. She just went on like that and the doctor nodded his head, rubbing his jaw, saying, 'Even if she wakes I don't know. I don't know.'

Uncle Godfrey disappeared up the stairs. Maxine poured a tumbler of milk and followed him up. *Mother wraps her coat tighter as she stands in the long grass by the shore. 'Has no one told you to come out?' I say nothing. She'll vanish if I even say one word. No one has told me. No one.* She opened her eyes. It was her uncle speaking, standing where she would have to pass to get out of the water and dry herself off.

'Well? Do you think it sensible to stand out there in your clothes and daydream?' Stubble darkened his jaw line. His eye sharpened on her. She couldn't think of something to say, so she started making her way to the shore. He turned away from her and marched back towards the gate through which he had first come.

'You'll have to grow up, my girl. My word you will.' But it was as if he wasn't speaking to her. He slammed the gate behind him and she heard the rattle again, the ringing of the bell.

As she stood on the shore the water running off her, the house looking down on her, a green light settled on everything; it was dusk and she was cast in shadows from the harbour and the trees. She towelled herself down with a woollen shawl she'd left in the grass and began to shiver; she couldn't see Maxine, so made her way to the kitchen door and called out. Maxine appeared in a rush from a side room off the laundry where she went for fire wood.

'Look at you. Go upstairs and get changed, for God's sake. I can't cope with both of you in a state...' She stopped and screwed up her face. With a flick of her arm, she pointed to the door and, behind it, the stairs that led up to Mathilde's room. *The housekeeper heard the roar of a great fire erupting behind her. She turned. And cried out.*

Mathilde went through the door and Maxine followed her. *She ran into the house, hearing the cries of the children.* Her imagination carried on, even though she was out of the water. The older woman disappeared for a moment as Mathilde paused at the kitchen table, and returned with an enormous towel. The girl dried herself off.

'Can I sit here now?' said Mathilde.

'As long as you're dry enough. I can't stop you.' Maxine turned to the stove, glaring. 'God knows what you do out there.'

'Maxine, tell me how old you are? Will you tell me?'

Maxine laughed. 'Exactly twice your age.'

'So you're thirty years of age. We'll be this way forever, you know.'

Maxine paused for a moment, then shook her head and said, 'Yes. But you say the strangest things.'

'I hope before I get to your age my hair changes colour and I'm as blonde as you are right now.'

The housekeeper turned to the girl. *How strange. The poor child.* 'When you're as old as me, love,' she said, 'you'll have hair as dark and as beautiful as your mother's.'

It was almost night, so Maxine turned to the door and switched on the bulb that was suspended over the table. *The youngest child she carries under her arm, the other grips her tightly around the neck, balancing on her hip.*

'Now go get yourself changed.'

Mathilde picked herself up and went through the door and towards the stairs. Maxine watched her go, turning her head, then once the girl was gone, bent down to return the pots she'd been drying back to the cupboard. A dull pain broke out along her back. That girl, she thought. That poor girl. She adjusted her weight awkwardly. The Uncle had pushed past her, but what could she say? What right did she have to stand in his way? He was determined, and glaring. She knew that one day he would come for the child and that she'd cry her eyes out, but there would be nothing she would do, no way to stand him aside. She knew that look about a man; the way he walked with a pace about him, a forward inertia, and his eyes that bore down on you with their unseeing darkness. She knew that look. All they ever see, she thought, all his eyes ever contemplate is that something is in his way. Mathilde would be going, she knew it. Don't stand in the way, don't even be here. She could hear the girl above her, going through her drawers, closing the doors heavily behind her. A draught ruffled the hem of her apron and she shivered; could she stand with her open palms on the man's chest and shock him into seeing her, into seeing what he was doing? Could she show him what the girl really was; a child lost in the books that lined her shelves and covered her floor and which were stacked in two feet high piles around her bed? Maxine's chest leapt when Mathilde had sat in the kitchen with her little fingers turned around a cloth volume and had read four words of the title with no help. This had been years before. She thought of that moment again as she served the meal onto two plates and set them on the table. She heard Mathilde's bare feet on the stairs and then the girl appeared, her face red from warm water and her thin body wrapped in a grey woollen blanket.

'Mathilde,' said the housekeeper, 'I hope you're wearing something under that. Something warm. How will you eat with that on?'

'I can't bear soup.' The girl laughed. 'You'll feed it to me.'

Maxine huffed. Those days were gone.

In the morning, thought Mathilde, early, even before Maxine is awake, I will swim. Get back out into the water. Since warming herself in a bowl of hot water, it was harder to make up the tales that amused her, the ones that came so easily when she stood in the harbour. Perhaps this is growing up, she thought; spending every thought on all the trouble that was in a circle drawn ten feet around them and forgetting the extraordinary possibilities, the luminescent networks that radiate outwards, like the ripples she stirs up in the slow paced water. *The children hold her tightly; she'll never let them go.*

'Are we going to class tomorrow?' said Mathilde. She was sitting at the table then, spooning soup up to her mouth and grimacing.

'You can't tell a soul. What would your uncle say if he found out? That would be the end of both of us. So you can just keep your trap shut about that. And yes, tomorrow afternoon we'll go. I don't mind if you come.' Maxine looked down at her hands; she knew it was a mistake. 'Isn't there something you should be learning at school instead?'

Mathilde laughed. The rooms of the old house thundered with it. 'Children, silence!' she shouted in mockery. 'Fingers on home row keys. Ready? Type!' Maxine laughed, too. Mathilde was standing now, arranging the fruit bowl in the centre of the table, placing the apples and pears either side of the two tropical mangos. 'Why don't you paint these instead? I could do this for you. I'd arrange all the fruit for you, see?' She put the empty soup bowl down beside the arrangement of fruit. 'It's a masterpiece. Now all you have to do is paint it.'

'Oh, and that is really nothing at all, is it. Tomorrow I think we have a model.'

'A real live model?' The girl clapped his hands together. 'A naked lady.'

'Well, I hope she'll have some clothes on. I'll be shy otherwise.'

'I'll laugh. I'll roar with laughter. Oh, paint her with a beard, won't you? I'll laugh so hard I'll die.' While she spoke she moved the still life around the table. She piled the fruit up, and removed it, making her own idea of what a canvas should look like.

'I'm going to light a cigarette,' said the housekeeper, going through a drawer; she found the packet, pulled out a length and lit it with a match. She breathed it in deeply, letting the smoke excoriate her.

'Why do you do that? Mother said it is a filthy habit.' *The children clung to her legs, leaving bruises, while she drew the smoke in deep. No. This won't work.* 'But I suppose there's a reason.'

'Why does anyone do anything?' The girl shrugged so the housekeeper went on. 'It's a habit. I suppose at one time it felt good. Don't you think it makes me look modern?'

Mathilde laughed.

'Well you're not exactly old.'

'Not exactly. Thank you. So charming.' She finished the cigarette.

'Please, dear, not a word.'

Mathilde nodded. 'I wouldn't spoil it.'

They tidied the table, resetting the disarranged fruit bowl, then washing the dishes. Mathilde wet a cloth and wiped down the table. As she ran the cloth over the surface, she thought again of the water rippling around her. They were cool, the hands that gripped her, covering her thighs, stretching around her waist.

After she'd kissed Maxine good night, she drifted up to her bedroom, pausing at her mother's door. The woman lay as if in state, with a cloth over her eyes. Mathilde couldn't bring herself to go in the room. She knew she should go in, but she remembered sitting on the edge of the bed, when her mother was still conscious; she opened her eyes, barely, and there was a glimmer. 'Your birthday. It was your birthday.' Mathilde didn't care. She just wanted the woman to stir, to swing her legs over the edge of the bed. 'I'll fix you up for that.' She slipped away again, all in a hurry. That was the last thing she said.

Mathilde fell asleep, but sleep was a broken and diffuse thing. She wasn't under the covers, but still dreamed. A breeze moved the sheer curtains in her room, and cooled her. In her sleep, she pulled her woollen cardigan tighter, then searched around the bed for a blanket, which remained folded up at her feet. There was a man leaning over her, his face she remembered, or that felt inside like a collision. She said his name in her sleep, or at least what she once called him, which now she couldn't recall, not in the depths of the sleep that covered her like a coloured but transparent film. She stirred, rising up a little on her elbow. There was a memory, the feeling of him, of being carried in his arms, was all recoiled in her muscles. These images merged with her a dream of her mother. She stirred; it was all was forgotten, not forbidden, just separated from her. It was sweat that covered her. Now, less than half awake, she remembered the bundle she made in his arms as he'd carried her down the stairs and the shouting and crying of his mother. Then she was sitting in a chair by the door, her head hung and her face red and wet. She knew crying, even then, or felt it, while she held a wooden toy tight to herself. She stirred with all of this, feeling it moving through her like a hand passing through water. It was substantial, a solid mass; she was nothing, just the displacement of a slippery mess. *The woman couldn't stop the man taking the child. He threw her down to her knees and she knew it was right. That the man would take the child, that he would carry the bundle into the front seat of the car and disappear.* She remembered shouting, how slight her mother had looked, but how he put the child down, put his hand on its cheek and said, 'Don't worry Mathilde. I won't ever be too far away.'

Then she was awake to the pitch of her room, the window that held the harbour glimmer, and so she thought, a distance; which way would it go if she could draw a line from her to him. *Direction was the least of it.* Never too far, she thought, but far enough.

She lay down and straightened out her body, drawing up the covers. Don't think about it, she told herself. Don't even think.

When she woke, the light came in blunt and early, like the embers of what had been brewing the night before. Somewhere in the house the house-keeper was running about, humming, singing, as she arranged and rearranged. Mathilde heard the car, pulling in to the drive. She knew the sound of it now, the open throated rumble as it came to a stop as close to the front door as possible. From her window she could see the driver's door, but not the driver. The passenger's door opened, then slammed shut and she saw her aunt, not her uncle, move quickly around the car and barrel towards the house.

Her aunt loomed from a shadow beside the car, that woman she despised, gathering around her the hem of a sun dress, and a gravity that Mathilde could feel, even watching her from the bedroom window of the first floor. The woman glared. She carried an enormous hat in her hands. Maxine became quiet, hearing the car, then Mathilde heard her other door. Her head came through and smiled.

'Not a sound. It's 9:30. You should be at school. She'll go wild if she finds you here.'

Mathilde waved the housekeeper away and whispered, 'Yes, go.' Then the housekeeper was gone. Somewhere below, the door opened and she heard her aunt's voice, pitched and complaining. She couldn't make out the words. *Her aunt held her hand open, raised above the girl who stood defiantly.* Raised voices came up the stairs, then the aunt's deft feet. She opened the door, and Mathilde stiffened, pulling up the sheet, covering her neck.

'You're indulged,' said the aunt. 'When you're mine, there'll be none of this.' Mathilde said nothing. The older woman approached the bed, crossing her arms. 'Laying in bed,' she said. 'While you should be in school.' The girl looked. 'Do you know what I do for a living?' The girl shook her head. 'I'm not a housemaid.'

'You're a lawyer.'

The aunt nodded. 'I look at things like this. There are some men I ruin, and others whose fortunes I help build. All in all, that's bad news for anyone standing in the way. And you and your mother...' The girl didn't flinch. 'When was the last time she spoke?'

'Why would you care about that? You care for so little.'

'Of course I care.'

'You barely looked at her when she wasn't sick. I remember, I was there watching.'

The aunt paused, setting her mouth and resetting it, moving her lips together. 'It will become even harder for you. You can't understand all of it, you're only a child, but there are many ways that I can help you.' Mathilde sat up in the bed, her muscles tensing. The aunt went on. 'There's a phrase I use in practice. I use it whenever I deliver news to a client that I know will destroy them. I say very slowly, "I regret so much that I am the one who must tell you this." Then I tell them. Can you understand why I am telling you this?' The girl looked down. Her face had softened. It was less defiant. The aunt shifted her weight, thinking twice about saying it. 'You'll need my help, that's why. When she passes — I can barely even say it — when she goes, I will be here. But first you must tell me when she last spoke. The woman can't sign her name now, can she? We'll have to fix things up.'

Mathilde didn't flinch. *The woman held her raised hand open, and the girl didn't flinch.* 'I wouldn't tell you, not ever. I think you're a monster.' The aunt laughed, drew herself slowly to full height, then turned to the door. She stopped for a moment, looking back at the girl, then thought better of speaking. She pulled the door closed sharply behind her.

Still in bed, Mathilde was exhausted, not moving, letting sleep grab her, then let her go. The housekeeper was nowhere in the house, or at least Mathilde couldn't hear her, just the harbourside sounds at midday, the lazy rustling of a lawnmower and the breeze that would rise in the leaves and then quicken and then within minutes die. She closed her eyes and couldn't even imagine the aunt's face anymore. *The old woman lost her features, her mouth was a hole that wouldn't close. The girl who laughed as her aunt disappeared.* In the drawer next to her bed she found a watch. She was still coming in and out of sleep. It was midday by the time her body loosened at the thought of the class that would start, the arrangement of the still life. She yawned. The sound of the aunt's car had startled her and the thoughts of her mother, still alive, lying in the way of her sister's money. The light raged on around her, and, flat out in a sleep that was as black as a hole in the sister's face, Mathilde thought she could see contortions that were like laughter, but something close and fixed. Damn the housekeeper, and how tired she felt, drawn up beneath all the cotton and wool, in a paralysis that held her between its thumb and forefinger. She should lift herself up and walk down the hall and crawl into the bed next to her mother, she should draw the last warmth from her, take that at least from the dying woman. There was nothing, not even this, and now Maxine was in the room, pulling at her shoulders and talking about painting and the colour wheel that was just as important. *Maxine stood at the easel but couldn't paint, there was nothing in her brush, her wrist was stiff.* The girl felt the heat but wouldn't move. *She stood up and the bed clothes fell away from her, and the sweat dried on her neck, all down her back, in the folds beneath her breasts. She stood still, naked. She heard her mother downstairs in the kitchen, boiling water in a saucepan to make her tea.* The housekeeper was at her door now, looking in on her. 'C'mon. Don't worry about it, dear. Let's get dressed and go. You need to get your fingers into the paint.'

The room was unsettled by the swathe the aunt had cut through it. She was automatic, pulling herself up, pulling a shirt on over her arms, over her shoulders. Nothing made sense in the way she moved, but the housekeeper stood there, looking over her, pulling her on, frowning because Mathilde didn't speak. 'Don't pay attention to her, dear. Soon your mother will be better; then really nothing will worry you. But still. Let's go, quick.' Mathilde followed her out the door, on to the street and waited for the bus into the city. She looked at the housekeeper, watched her, saw her impatience.

When the bus appeared, Mathilde said, 'Alright. I'm sorry, I'm with you now. There's the bus.'

It was half an hour before they were inside the studio. *It was how I imagined, but I was quiet, pushing myself up against the wall at the back.* A table spread out with a red cloth and a bowl of fruit. A bottle full of water, and an empty glass. Maxine stood at the easel, mixing paint. Mathilde counted out four women, all around Maxine's age; when they noticed her, each of them smiled in turn. A door opened at the front, near where the still life they were meant to paint had been arranged (Mathilde couldn't work who had arranged it). A woman in a white robe, the model, came in. Mathilde kept an eye on her as she pulled up a canvas chair. She draped herself over it, slouching into it. If Mathilde could've painted anything, perhaps she would've painted the way the model looked over the studio in her bored, detached way.

'I'm just happy watching you now,' Mathilde said to Maxine. Maxine was moving the paint around a board, mixing the colours. They're too dark, thought Mathilde. If they'd been hers she would brighten them. Oranges and blue for the orange to strike against. And a kind of purple. Or white alone against black. She stretched, watching as they worked, then thought of the minutes that passed, tipping themselves out like loose change on the bus. She saw Maxine's hands, moving on the face of the board, moving a red paint across it after sketching out her dimensions in pencil. *I stand up; it's the boredom I cannot bear. I want to see them strike out with colour, to see come off them in a shower of sparks. To cover the walls in colour. Nothing waits as patiently as I do.*

A breeze was blowing into the door that led onto the street at the back. She went to it and pushed it open. A gust came in and she saw all the faces look at her. She spoke just to Maxine. 'I'm just going to wait outside for a while, I think.' Maxine frowned, but said nothing, so the girl slipped out onto the street.

It was tiresome standing in the one spot. She walked a little further away, pushing herself faster, into the cool air; she thought about her part of the harbour and would have liked to stand neck deep in the water, moving it around her, forcing it. The city street came at her, all the faces she didn't recognise, but perhaps should have; how could there be so many people, none of whom she recognised? She counted over a dozen. *I've been seeing these people all my life. There are faces I don't know, but I know that. What should I care? All the faces, like fruit arranged on a table.* She made her way down to the bridge, and sat with her back against one of its enormous cold grey feet. She rested there, not closing her eyes, but not seeing. Oh the life, the boredom. She clenched her fists. All she wanted was to stand in the water.

She saw a boy, a few years younger perhaps, darting into her peripheral vision. She turned to him. He said, 'I saw you come out of that place.' He pointed. 'Are you lost?' It was a boy like she hadn't seen before, dressed like a man, his face grimy, but with eyes that were wide and burning. He wore a coat with holes in the elbows and a red cloth around his neck, not to keep him warm. 'You shouldn't stay around here. A little girl all alone. Where's your mother then?'

'I'm with my housekeeper. She's in there, painting.'

'Painting what?' There was a look in his eye, then he laughed. He stuck

out his hand at her, as though he was fully grown. 'My name is Lenny.'
She didn't take his hand, but watched him as he started to twitch. It was
as if he was releasing all the accumulated energy. Then he was dancing
in front of her, not looking at her anymore, moving his feet, making
squares with them, kicking up dirt and grass, but unable to stay still.

Mathilde watched him, drawn to him. He pulled a large patchwork
handkerchief from his pocket, lay it down neatly next to her, and sat on
it. 'What's your name, little girl? Of course you have one.'

'Of course,' she said. 'Mathilde.' She stuck out her hand and he shook
it.

'You must be lost,' said Lenny. 'I mean, look at you. You don't belong,
not even here. I bet you don't belong there either.'

'No. I don't. It must be obvious. But watch your mouth.'

'It's just the age you're at, that's all. When I'm your age, I'll be just the
same, sitting out here by myself.'

She felt that none of it was real. Could there be a place like this? The
colours were still bright. Lenny looked carefully at her. How had he just
appeared? He took an apple from his coat pocket.

'I only have one,' he said.

'I don't care. Eat whatever you like, I'm not hungry.'

He devoured it. The sun was bright on it, she thought, bearing down.
She would've painted him, in his threadbare coat and tattered red scarf,
his back against the stone foot of the bridge.

'I don't know where my mother is, either,' he said. 'Nor the old man.
He was a miner. I had a book with pictures of a mine, once. Not inside,
but you know. All that black and white dirt, charred trees sticking up
and all their arms and legs and their faces were so black.' Lenny looked
at her, but vacantly; he was seeing through her, still considering the
apple he was chewing.

'Let's walk down to the water,' he said. 'It's where I always wind up.'
He leapt to his feet and grabbed her wrists, pulling her up as well. She
laughed and, hearing this, he swung her around, putting his hand on
her waist as though they were dancing. Everything whirled. She threw
back her head and saw the gunmetal sky.

'Oh, I feel like I can't stand straight,' she said.

'Then let's dance,' said Lenny. He lost his balance and they went
tumbling down the grassy incline, a knot of intertwined limbs. She was
still laughing when they stopped, but Lenny leapt up and glared at her,
brushing himself down. 'It comes to this, sooner or later. Your head

can't handle it and it hurts and all that's left is laughter.' She couldn't tell if he was serious.

'But I'm not laughing at you,' she said. 'I'm just laughing.'

'Either way,' he said, 'Let's go down to the water.' He turned his back and started marching.

'But I can't move,' she called to him, still laughing. *For a moment she is aware that she is flat on her back, the blanket pulled up to her neck. She reaches up, hears her mother's voice. Her eyes are not the same, not like they were.* She thought of Maxine searching the house, calling her name; Maxine arranging her paints on the palette and preparing the brushes. She thought of her mother, what it was to be motionless, out of breath. Lenny took her hand. His palm was cool on hers. She followed.

'We can walk around to my house if you like. My mother's there. She's not well. She hasn't woken up.'

'What's wrong with her?' Lenny asked.

'It's an interesting case. That's what the doctors say.' She gripped his hand tighter. He said nothing, only raised his eyebrows. 'A type of meningitis. They don't really know for sure.'

'And she won't wake up.'

Mathilde didn't know, not really. They followed a road away from the bridge, walking down a street that was lined with flats and plane trees. Lenny skipped every third or fifth step and she laughed, stumbling, still trying to hold on to him.

'Well,' he said, 'never mind. At least you like music.' She tripped and he skipped again, then she heard the dull pounding of drums and a pressure behind her eyes. She turned the corner. She could see her house. The first thing she always looked at was the window of the room where her mother was. She walked faster and this time Lenny didn't trip. *The water reared up into sight as though it was rushing towards us and we weren't moving, but were fixed into a place beside the road.*

'Do you like the theatre? Wait. I know you do.' Such a strange question, she thought. But he was right. 'When I grow up,' he said, 'I'll be on the stage.'

Mathilde followed the road down to the water's edge, walking on the soft dirt that spilled over onto the bitumen where the curb should've been. Grass grew on the verge, along with a lengthy belt of weeds. She stopped for a moment and imagined closing her eyes and dipping her fingers in music that she imagined flowing past. She looked harder at the house. Behind her Lenny waited. He watched her make her way down to the water. She looked back and saw he was waving at her, his arms furious. She did. She closed her eyes.

Then she was out into the harbour, stirring it around her, getting lost in it. You should paint like this, she thought. It's like carrying yourself up into the sky, feeling the weight fall away. Somewhere behind her, was her mother. *She stood at the top of the stairs and looked. I waited for her to speak, to break the motionlessness that had settled within her bones.* Was Lenny still there? She looked back, and saw the car pulling into the drive, her uncle was driving and, next to him, the shadow of what must've been her aunt. She turned back to the water, submerged, cold, but feeling everything about the world seeping into her. She could cry out and the sky would ring with it. It would be like a choir, the voice she would have released. She lost herself completely for a moment, was drawn under.

Then the voice of the aunt. 'Shake her, Godfrey. Hit her on the back. You're alright, you know. You're tough.' Was she on a bed? Was she lying back against something soft and collapsing? She tried to lift her arms up, up out of the water. The music she imagined was louder, but she was still deep in the cold water. It was grey, the colour her blue eyes go when her head pounds. She thought of this because of the vague ache behind her eyes, the drumming. She opened them and saw Maxine by the door crying.

'She's alright,' said the aunt. The maid's sobbing wracked her body, folded her up. 'She's delirious, But we need to warm her up.'

The uncle's hands pulled her up by the collar, dragged her up through the brine. She heard his voice, shouting to the aunt who was standing on the bank with her arms crossed. The uncle was deep in the water; it was well up past his waist. As she struggled, he stirred the mud up around them. She came up into the air and heard the aunt, calling out again. *My mother comes out into the water, the hem of her summer dress floating on the surface.* There was a darkness to the light, she noticed. The green of the plane trees was tinged by a blue. 'It's alright, love,' said her uncle as she gave in. He gathered her up into a bundle he could just fit into the circumference of his arms. He walked with her towards the shore.

'Where is she?' she asked him.

'Who, dear? You almost drowned.' She was shaking her head. She could see. A fury rose again inside her, filling the inside of her mouth. She wasn't confused anymore and stared at the eyes on the aunt who stood glaring. She'd stopped looking for her mother. For a moment she struggled, then again surrendered. *I pull myself free, my legs like pistons, driving me up into the light, which is obscured by the Moreton Bay near the road. I can see her looking on, glad that I can swim.* She coughed, spitting out a salty mouthful. The aunt glared, thinking she had won, but Mathilde turned away from her and kicked until her uncle dropped her. She landed on her side in the shallows, but struggled quickly to her feet, and ran, her feet sinking into the mud then finding the grass when she was out of the water. She couldn't see Lenny, but she put her head down and flew, taking the direction she had in her, aligned with a trajectory only her body knew how to take. It was a line away from them. *I see him in the distance, where he's stopped. He was receding away, with the light. I'll keep running, that's the way to catch him, with a fire at my heels. There are muscles, nerves in my legs that take me.*

Lenny still waved to her, hidden near the road, wild that she had walked out into the water, where he was afraid to go. He'd ducked behind a tree when the car pulled up. He put his hands wide apart when she fell and started running. Then he laughed, so loud she could hear it. Part of her wanted to go back, to run towards Maxine, who she could see from the corner of her eye was also moving towards her. She wanted to feel the old boards of the house beneath her feet, to emerge into the empty space and turn her face up to the roof, to see the lights and the cobwebs of its sharp corners. But she didn't need to see it; she already knew. She already imagined it. Lenny began to dance and she laughed. She forget her mother, whatever it was the aunt was shouting, and the maid as well. Yes, she thought. Maxine and her still life. With her brushes bearing down on them all. Mathilde, she said to herself. Don't stop yet. Let your legs take you. And memory of her hands moving in the water pulled her in as deep as it pleased. And she went faster towards him. As fast as she could manage, to where she couldn't see the shore, or the aunt. She was close to Lenny now, where she could see the coloured squares that he stuffed into his top pocket and his red scarf, and where there was the overflow of colours, and a depth, a block of dissected light reflected onto the canvas.

Miro Sandev

Zugswang

two figures stand head
  to head in a square
room after the attrition,
in a kind of staring contest

the distractions of the minor
pieces amuse no longer;
both parties are
stripped bare as a bride

memory is the chequered map
that lies at their feet tattered
but not so badly torn as
to rule out talk
of the best route

the only spectators:
two clocks on either side

next to move loses

Helga Jermy

Jury Duty

We're through *voir dire*,
with all our faults and limitations,
the evidence before us is a lengthy
brief (an altercation, beer
and bias, a skull's white cupped
frailty cracked against a wall)
and we're just peers peering in on
back stares of discomfort, wondering
if the kids are home from school,
if the paintings reached the gallery,
if last night's Tuscany pork will stretch
to a kind of cassoulet, then graphic
piercings to inattention, cuts
through flesh and bone, seething
words spat with such ferocity
that DNA is found in an eye socket,
knuckles smashed into brick a bloody
signature underwriting one more loss,
and the tight knot in my stomach is
another twisted gristle punch of revenge.

Chris Palazzolo

The Woodies

1.

When Aaron Kendal showed paramedics Beezley and Crowe to his mother's bedroom, they wondered at first why they'd been called. A short, stooping woman in her sixties, dressed in a floral dress, fawn cardigan and sensible brown shoes, stood pole-still at the foot of her neat double bed. It looked like nothing more serious than a woman, paused from her chores, lost in a reverie involving her bedroom curtains.

'Is this your mum?' Beezley snapped, unable to hide his annoyance.

Aaron nodded. Beezley studied his frightened little eyes, smelt the sweat and piddle of chronic prostatitis coming off his clothes, noted the unshaven face bloated with medication, and thought, ANR (Ambulance Not Required).

Still, better make sure.

'Hello Mrs Kendal,' he called with forced good humour. 'Mrs Kendal?' The woman didn't move.

Crowe stepped cautiously around the bed towards her.

'Mrs Kendal?' she cooed. 'Hellooo, Mrs Kendal? Are you alright?'

She waved her hand in front of Mrs Kendal's face. No response. She looked up her colleague and shrugged.

'She's been like that for an hour,' Aaron said.

'Mrs Kendal, come on.' Crowe gently placed her hand on Mrs Kendal's shoulder.

With a quick yelp she jerked her hand away as if it had touched an electric fence, and froze for a second, her hand held up. She touched the shoulder again. Her hand jerked back. Quickly, with both hands, she felt the woman's chest and shoulders, then turned and marched back up to her colleague, hands clenching and unclenching, trying to rake in some professional composure.

'She's hard!' she whispered to Beezley.

'She's what?'

'She's hard!' she hissed in his ear. 'She's stiff as a board!'

'What?' Aaron said 'What's the matter?'

Crowe pushed Beezley towards Mrs Kendal. 'Feel her.'

'What's the matter?' Aaron whined. 'What are you talking about?'

Beezley peered into the woman's eyes. The light brown irises appeared almost dusty.

'She's catatonic.' He touched her shoulder, but his hand jerked back and he stepped back in shock, whistling and clapping his hands. He quickly felt her cheeks, neck, chest and shoulders, then put a stethoscope on and pressed it to her chest.

'She's alright isn't she?' Aaron pleaded. 'She's gonna be alright?'

'How long has she been like this?' Crowe asked.

'About an hour.'

'And you found her here like this?'

'No, she was in the kitchen. I brought her in here so she could lie down.'

'Aaron, I'm gonna have to ask you to leave the room for a while,' Beezley said.

'There's something wrong with her isn't there?'

Crowe gently took his arm. 'Aaron, we need you to go out of the room, okay. Sit down and wait.'

'Why? What's wrong?'

'We don't know yet. Now please, I need to talk to my colleague.'

She ushered him out the room and closed the door.

'There's no heartbeat,' Beezley said. Crowe listened with her stethoscope.

'What should we do? Try CPR?'

Beezley pinched the top of his lip.

'She's cold. She's stiff.'

He took a penlight out of his pocket and shined it in Mrs Kendal's eyes.

'Eyes are dry. Pupils fixed and dilated.'

He flicked the light off and looked at Crowe.

'She's dead.'

Crowe stared at him.

'But she can't be dead, she's still standing!'

They looked down at her feet. Beezley squatted and felt the woman's calves, smelling the concentrated urine that had dried on her thighs.

'Her legs are normal, warm and supple.'

He pressed with his fingers up the woman's leg until he found the line of stiffness just above the pelvis. Crowe did the same and together they traced the circumference of the ridge where the skin became as hard as leather on a cricket ball.

'Let's lie her on the bed,' Beezley said.

A miserable snotty moaning began outside the bedroom door, rising to a wail of panicked grief as the paramedics worked. They carefully lay Mrs Kendal on the bed.

The woman's legs came to life as soon as they stepped back, kicking up and around and pulling the weight of her body over the edge of the bed. With a tremendous swaying effort, she stood up again, her feet taking a couple of heavy steps, before finding balance, the top half of her body completely stiff, swaying.

'Well,' Beezley muttered, pinching his lip again. 'She's not dead.'

His vision clouded because he'd forgotten to blink.

2.

Detective Sergeant Neil Capshaw hated things he didn't understand. As he bent forward, hands on knees, and stared at the poor old girl's legs, he felt the terrible futile anger that had ruined his marriage and alienated his children filling his head. The legs were trembling like mad and a reddish-purple bruise had formed around the swollen ankles.

'So why's she trembling then? Just tired from standing?'

Dr Ramasinga stood behind him, arms crossed. A young constable took photos of Mrs Kendal and the bedroom with a digital camera. The door was marked off by a diagonal strip of yellow tape.

'Oh yes I should think so,' Ramasinga said. 'You see that bruising. That is happening now as we are watching. If the top half of her body is dead, then it is just an inert mass that's sitting on top of her legs. I mean it's the same weight as when it was alive. But a living body is always moving and adjusting and counterbalancing in such a way as to minimise stress on the legs and feet. I don't know if you understand that...'

The precise nervous tones made Capshaw's mind flash. He rounded on the poor doctor as if he was about to punch his lights out.

'No, I don't! Call me stupid, but I seem to be missing something! If her legs are alive, and the rest of her body is dead. Then where's the ff-effing blood circulation and the effing nerve impulses coming from!'

'Well, th-th-that was my o-original point. She's not dead. Ob-obviously the exterior organs of the top half of her body have become a shell and everything inside is still working.'

'Ob-obviously,' Capshaw sneered. He was scared. Twenty years in the force and for the first time ever he was scared. This is it, he thought. The thing every policeman dreads: witnessing something so repulsive he'll take it to the grave.

'Uh oh, here she goes!' He couldn't hide the terror in his voice, he couldn't stop himself stepping back. Because Mrs Kendal's legs had finally buckled. She fell on her knees with a ghastly THOMP! Arms still stiff at her sides she started to keel forward. Ramasinga and the constable leapt forward to catch her before her face hit the floor. Lying her down gently, Ramasinga instinctively tried to turn her head to the side, but it was completely rigid. For a moment she was motionless. Then her legs began sliding and kicking around trying to find traction to get up.

Capshaw knew his mind was stained.

'She never bloody gives up.'

3.

Dr Graham Porter MBBS, Fellow of the Royal Australasian College of Surgeons, was Director of Clinical Services at the Central _____ Hospital. Only the most serious cases of injury or contagious illness required him to come down to the wards, don the mask and gloves and do an examination. When he entered the isolation ward with treating physician Dr Michael McDowell, he observed that the woman lying on the examination table was either dead or in a deep coma: her eyes were wide open staring unblinking up at the harsh fluorescents. Two junior doctors, Cho and Roy, in gowns and masks, stood a metre away from the table.

'Okay doctor,' Porter said. 'What's the story? Keep it brief. There's some crisis in the Emergency Department I have to attend to.'

'I think it'll be best, sir, if you first feel the patient.'

Porter touched Mrs Kendal's arm and chest, then leant over and took a cursory glance at her eyes.

'She's dead doctor. Probably been dead for two days.'

'She's not dead, sir.'

'Well then what is it?'

McDowell coughed. 'Well, basically, sir, you'll, probably, find this hard to believe, but...'

His sentence broke off. He looked over at the two junior doctors helplessly.

'Well come on then,' Porter snapped.

'Well.' McDowell coughed again. 'Basically, all the external organs of the top half of her body from the waist up appear to have turned into a carapace of...wood.'

'Wood?'

'Yes sir, that's what it appears to be. All the internal organs seem to be normal and functioning. We... We drilled a hole through the lower thorax and inserted a scope.'

He lifted up a cut flap of Mrs Kendal's dress and showed Porter the neat drilled hole.

Porter stared at the faint strata of rings in the wall of the hole.

'Doctor, I'm not sure I understand.'

'We don't understand either, sir,' McDowell spoke hurriedly now. 'We cut a section off her right earlobe and had it examined, and the closest material we can find to it is, wood. The skin, the flesh, the eyes seem to have metamorphosed into wood. She is basically a hollow wooden doll from the waist up, with a functioning brain, lungs and blood system inside.'

Porter was far too experienced to let his professionalism be shaken. He proceeded to examine the woman. He stroked her hair, and experienced a thrill of unprofessional horror when a dry clump came off the scalp and crumbled into ashen dust through his fingers.

'As you can see sir, she's still got nostrils.'

Porter examined the open holes under the nose.

'Impossible!' He pressed the rigid chest. 'How is she drawing the air in?'

'The diaphragm appears to enjoy a limited flexibility.'

Porter continued probing, cheeks, neck, throat. 'Heart-rate?'

'Two beats every five seconds.'

'She's in a coma.'

He shined a penlight at the eyes. They looked like burnished knots of pine set in the wooden sockets by some master woodcarver.

'God be praised for tiny mercies,' he whispered. 'A conscious brain sealed in that.'

'If you examine the legs sir, you will notice they are quite normal.'

Porter felt the legs.

'They feel cold and hard to me, doctor.'

McDowell frowned. He clutched one of the legs and his face turned white.

'This must have happened in the last ten minutes! Did you notice anything?!'

The junior doctors shook their heads, their eyes wide with terror.

'I want this floor quarantined,' Porter announced. 'We don't know if this condition is contagious. Who else knows about this?'

'Apart from us here, only the emergency personnel that brought her in.'

'Okay, I want it to stay like that. I don't want anyone uttering a word, especially to those journalists downstairs. Something is happening in Emergency. I don't know if it has anything to do with this or not. But this must remain strictly secret until we know more about what we're dealing with.'

He turned to Cho and Roy. 'I want you two to stay here. You can wait outside if you prefer. No one is to enter this room. We'll be back in fifteen minutes. Doctor, if you'll come with me.'

Porter and McDowell left. The two junior doctors hurriedly took chairs out to the corridor and sat. The fluorescent-lit corridor was cold and hushed, and Roy clutched his shoulders for warmth staring longingly at the lift at the far end.

'Are they going to get a saw?' he said to his reticent colleague. 'Saw the lady in half. Get it? Like a magic trick.'

Cho said nothing. In fact he was so still, if it wasn't for his blinking eyes Roy would've thought he'd turned to wood too.

With a big sigh that echoed down the corridor he rested his head on the wall. There was always the risk something like this would happen. Working twelve hour shifts, skipping breakfast and lunch, subsisting on evening meals in order to pay off debt. And here he was, stuck in isolation for heaven knows how long, scared, cold and dizzy with hunger.

The lift at the end of the corridor dinged, and Roy's hopes leapt at the thought of being relieved. But instead of doctors, three rough men wearing coloured anoraks and worksite fluoros exited. Cho and Roy jumped to their feet.

'I'm sorry, you can't come in here, this area's quaran…'

Roy's voice trailed off. The three men were filthy and deformed, the arm of one stuck out immobile like the branch of a tree, and another had a big hunch behind his neck which pushed his head sideways. Their clothes and grim faces were spattered with what looked like fresh blood. The two doctors shrunk back against the wall, almost swooning at the reek of sweat, shit and wet ash that surrounded the men like a cloud. The men ignored them and banged through the door of the isolation room. After a moment, they exited carrying Mrs Kendal like a log. The doctors stared in astonishment as the men carried her back to the lift and entered. The lift doors closed.

4.

SecureForce guard Ron Peeni was proud of the tattoos that narrated his past, and the Baptist faith that was the pillar of his present. But he'd bummed this one cigarette from his colleague Stokesy because something was happening. There were police and ambulance sirens everywhere. The two guards stood at the entrance of the Hospital's underground staff car-park, puffing anxiously. Someone was shouting from down the dark access lane, and Stokesy moved to the edge of the lane to try and hear.

'What's he saying?' Peeni called. 'Can you make it out?'

'Nup,' Stokesy said, peering into the gloom. 'Some gypo language.'

Another siren started up nearby, blue and red lights jabbing the evening gloom.

'What is it with all these fucken police sirens!' Stokesy shouted.

Peeni checked his phone again. Still dead. The last person he'd spoken to was his wife. That was nearly an hour ago. She'd told him the news reports of a couple of major crashes on the freeways. Perhaps these sirens were the wash-up. Though why his phone was dead too?

'What time is it?' Stokesy asked.

'Quarter past seven.'

'Some shit's goin' down eh.'

At that moment a white flash, like the flash of a camera bulb, lit up the laneway, followed, a split second later, by a bang so loud Peeni reeled, flinging his forearms across his face. At first his stunned mind thought gunshot, then quickly rationalised firecracker or car backfire. But when a thunderous aftershock clapped across the sky, momentarily drowning out the sirens, he knew something terrible was happening.

'Jeeesssuuuss Christ!' Stokesy cried. 'What the fuck was that!'

There were screams now, from the lane.

'Please don't blaspheme,' Peeni muttered.

Squealing tires suddenly echoed off the carpark walls. The two guards leapt out the way as a ute skidded down the ramp and sped off up the laneway. The three deformed men sat in the cabin, like a pot-bound knot of stiffening limbs, the man with the hunch driving. Mrs Kendal lay on the tray, sliding and bumping the sides as the ute swerved and sped up a city highway. Police and emergency vehicles were everywhere, tending car crashes and house fires on every street and intersection, flames and emergency flashes strobing the dark. Bewildered families stood on footpaths, packs of young men moved across the streets, their paranoid, terrified or laughing faces glimpsed in the headlights. Here and there, people had been set alight, flaming scarecrows running across front yards or through carparks pursued by police.

The freeway was unapproachable. Stationary cars and semi-trailers, many abandoned, some skewed and smouldering in pile-ups, blocked the flyover and all the entrances. Milling torchlights flickered along the edge of the freeway way out beyond the 100 zone.

The ute bumped up onto a verge and plunged into darkness, swerving perilously around trees and smashing through a wire and wooden fence before flying onto a potholed backroad heading deep into the ex-urban bush. After three kilometres it turned off the road and halted. Without shutting off the engine or switching off the headlights, the three men staggered out of the cabin, dragged Mrs Kendal off the tray and dumped her on the ground. They sat down nearby and went very still.

Sirens continued wailing in the distance.

5. (Eight Months Later)

Corporal Matthew Rydell was due some R&R. Resources were stretched so thinly his company was the only one detailed to search the north eastern suburbs for Woodies. For three long months he'd picked his way through trashed streets and burnt out shells of houses, demolishing walls, digging up gardens and bulldozing suburban reserves. In the last week the search had moved to the surrounding bushland where, not surprisingly, most have been found: clusters of them hidden under knolls and in ditches, or lying scattered near copses of trees and scrub. The day was dull and stifling as he trudged wearily over dry sticks and bramble, shirt off and tied around his waist, his sunburnt torso streaked with sweat and ash. The throat searing haze of burn hung in the air. He saw an abandoned ute under a circle of trees and quickened his pace towards it. There they were, the tell-tale clumps of deep fleshy green among the taupe and grey of banksia, melaleuca and Geraldton wax.

'Found some here!' he shouted to the rest of the platoon. 'One. Two three. Four foive!'

One of deep green bushes was Mrs Kendal. Her wooden legs stuck out of a knot of thick dark leaves. Her head was barely recognisable as human anymore. The contortions of growth had pushed the wooden tongue out so far the lips and cheeks had peeled back to form a rim around the ears. Three of the other bushes were the men who picked her up, and a fifth one, another Woody that had joined them after. They had become cribbed and deformed little trees, sprouting out uneven clumps of the fleshy leaves. Out of each of their eye-sockets had grown a stalk, on the end of which bloomed a grotesque flower with pulpy, triangular shaped petals secreting a pungent odour which resembled semen. The striations on the petals were the same colour as the eyeballs they'd erupted from: Mrs Kendal, a light pine brown; a couple of the others, blue.

For the soldiers it was more back-breaking labour. Using shovels and hatchets they dug wide holes around the trees to expose the white basketball-sized bulbs that had grown from the parts of the bodies that were touching the ground. Grunting, swearing, and hacking up gobs of black phlegm, they pulled the trees up with ropes.

Mrs Kendall and her four companions were taken to a nearby paddock and thrown onto a massive bonfire of alien trees. The plume of blue smoke rising into the sky merged with the smoke of hundreds of similar fires across the city, covering the sun in a filthy haze.

Norm Neill

march 1990, maid's day off

Nelson Mandela's release from gaol in February 1990 marked the beginning of the collapse of the apartheid system in South Africa.

Martha swears at the unwashed breakfast plates,
her maid for having Thursday off, her husband
(adequate income and incipient colitis)
for adultery, the dog for never barking,
the glass topped wall for sparkling in the sun
— and hurls the crockery across the kitchen floor.

Her nearest neighbours on each side turn down
the volume of their 'easy-listening' radios,
to trace the trouble's source, but realise
the violence is only psychological.
They sigh, pick up their glossy magazines,
sip cups of tea, and let the music soothe.

Martha checks the window locks, gulps down
a sugar-coated tranquilliser, glowers
at the gardener sharpening a blade, dark skinned
broad shouldered, squat, tight buttocked, young.
She opens up her bible, reads the day's set text,
Revelation 18, prays, and polishes her gun.

Frederick Pollack

Reception Theory

In the late work, we often see him
frantic to escape
the 'sealed room.' But when he opens
a door or window, he hesitates,
then closes it. Seldom writes
about love: it's where he
long since decided
to *live*, not think, not observe — at least,
not for public consumption.
As for 'nature,' his stance
resembles that of the old Jewess
in *Lacombe, Lucien*.
Improbably rescued from deportation,
tenuously safe
on a farm in the Midi, she is drawn,
one twilight, to a mysterious sound —
a cricket on a weed — and
bends to inspect it. It still pertains
to the goyim, the murderers
who claimed all space
for themselves; they can keep it.
He would rather invoke old movies.

Again and again in the late work,
spring leaves block
his view of a street. Should he use
'a street,' with its general appeal,
or insist on 'the Parkway across the river'
for its petty honesty?
The 'perfect' day, before humidity,
bugs, and the sweat
of the inert, is as much

a function of physics
as the sewage drowning Nashville,
the dying Gulf, the minds
of the BP spokesman and the Times Square bomber.
We see him, looking rather vacant, make
this note. We see him
remembering Hawking saying, 'I am free
in my mind.' (Discuss.)
What he wants is evidently
the sort of *advocacy* —
as-criticism one finds
in Sartre's essays of the Forties.

Sue Booker

When the Wind Blows

And he aſked him, What is thy name? And he anſwered, ſaying,
My name is Legion: for we are many.

At night my boyfriend and I go walking past the homes of the rich. He works days, and I'm hypersensitive to sunlight; a symptom of excess Vitamin D, my doctor gauged from my blood test. My boyfriend says you don't need to be rich, just mortgaged, to live in these fortresses. Still, I'd kill for their sea views, vast rooms and, not least, walls so thick they're soundproof. Barking is all we hear from their houses. And, in one case, unearthly grunts; but peering past the gate into the dark, we saw nothing.

When we turn the corner of my street on our way back, the lights are always on in the upstairs flat. They shine brighter than any nearby; the new tenant needs thicker curtains, or blinds. Yet, though she stays in nights, we've never seen her at the windows. I'd heard her resounding tread above my head for a month before I caught sight of her.

At last we passed each other on the stairs one day. Bouncy-haired and buxom, she's young to need subsidised housing; but so was I when my number came up.

'Hi,' she said, all smiles, eyes darting every which way. 'I'm Stacey.' And I'd barely said my name when she told me she'd left her spare key with my downstairs neighbour.

'Deb's your best bet,' I assured her, 'it's rare I can't hear her radio blasting —'

'Is my TV too loud?' Stacey asked. Hard to say, sounds merge, I answered. 'I leave it on all day,' she said, 'even when I'm not watching it —' my crack about her carbon footprint got no reaction — 'so just come up and knock if it's ever a problem! I don't notice things like that.'

My main peeve since she'd moved in, I confessed, was a frequent, hellishly dissonant squeaking. 'Is it your balcony door?' I said, my nostrils prickling; she smelled of smoke. 'It's never closed and the squeak always gets worse when the wind blows.'

Stacey shrugged. 'I don't think so, it's stopped with a brick…but,' she said, 'I'll try keeping it shut for the next month to see if that makes a difference.'

Once when I'd asked Deb at four a.m. to turn down her telly so I could sleep, she'd grizzled as if I'd disturbed *her* peace. So I thanked Stacey for her concern and returned to my flat feeling grateful.

That night, though, from the street below, my boyfriend and I saw her door gaping.

Go to, let us go down, and there confound their language,
that they may not underſtand one another's ſpeech.

My neighbours don't read; they fall quiet only while sleeping. Deb's telly or radio alternates with her strident voice, and Stacey keeps laundering, pacing her floor and, perversely often, flushing her toilet. I notice because I spend most of the day in bed. That's where I am on Mother's Day when I hear a knock. I close my King James Bible — a family heirloom from Mum's side — then lay it flat, on the floor by the mattress, to conserve the spine. My boyfriend's taken his mum out for brunch, so I have to get up. I squint through the peephole. 'Who is it?'

'Stacey!'

To shield her from the art on my walls, I open my door just a chink.

'Sorry it's so early,' she starts, though it must be past eleven, 'but could I borrow something to open this bottle? Want a glass? It's just cheap stuff, I got it on special for five dollars —'

'Thanks, but I only drink red.' I leave her on the landing while I fetch the corkscrew that looks like a legless little man with arms he can raise over his head.

'I'll bring it back later,' she says, taking it, but instead she sits on the stairs talking about aircraft noise and the pigeons while she twists the little man in. Is she avoiding her mother? Maybe when I heard Stacey before, she wasn't on the phone. Whole phrases float down when she speaks up; these blocks aren't called public housing for nothing. Yet in the two months she's lived above me I've never heard her ringtone. Nor did I hear her mother arrive, though my boyfriend was playing guitar for a while.

'Sure you don't want a glass?' Stacey holds up the mangled plastic stopper.

I'd as soon drink my own urine. 'Thanks but no, white wine gives me cystitis.'

She hands me the corkscrew. 'And my TV hasn't disturbed you?'

'Not like the squeaking,' I say, 'though that's worse on windy days —'

'Just come straight up and knock on my door the minute you hear it,' she says, 'and we'll see if we can find what's causing it?'

'Two heads are better than one,' I say, 'thanks heaps,' and I go back to bed, elated at the promise of relief. According to the free test I had, my hearing is well above average.

Aſk, and it ſhall be given you : ſeek, and ye ſhall find :
knock, and it ſhall be opened unto you.

Like the artist Frida Kahlo, I paint in bed, propped up with pillows. Not that I'm disabled, far from it, but we have screwed spinal columns in common. And, like Frida, I use myth and history. Both of which abound in my Bible. It even smells old, as did Great Aunt Ivy, who gave it to me when I was eleven, before doctors discovered what else I'd inherited.

Tonight, as I search its brittle, brown-edged, well-thumbed pages for inspiration, the noise overhead jangles my nerves. Like a child's swing in need of oiling but worse, it peals out with each breath of wind. At last I rise and pocket my key, then, hoping I won't interrupt her dinner, walk upstairs to Stacey's and knock.

'You heard it?' The whites of her eyes flash in the dimness. 'Come in!'

'I'm not disturbing you?'

'Not at all,' she says. 'Excuse the mess!' I glance around the draughty main room with its open windows and door, bare save for a portable telly and some clothes draped over a rack. The flimsy curtains flutter like flags. She points the remote and the screen goes black. Her eyes widen more. 'Did you hear that?'

We follow the sound to its source above the open kitchen window. 'So that's what it is — when the wind lifts the curtains the rods scrape the brackets,' I tell her.

'Blu-Tack,' she says. 'That should fix it. I'll buy some on Monday.'

That's four days from now. 'I've got some,' I say. 'Why don't I go and —'

'No,' she says, 'I'll get some on Monday and until then I'll keep the windows closed —'

'Thanks. That won't put you out,' I nod toward her washing, 'when the sound hasn't bothered you?'

'No, it's been annoying me too.' She's turned away so I can't see her face.

'Do you cop much noise from my flat?' I say.

'None, just the front door shutting —'

'You never hear my TV?'

'No, nothing reaches up this far —'

'You haven't heard me and my boyfriend argue?'

'Never. Just pigeons and planes and, like I was saying, everyone's doors...'

I smile to conceal a pang of envy and thank her again, then withdraw.

For all the law is fulfilled in one word, even in this;
Thou ſhalt love thy neighbour as thyſelf.

She sees me first, on her return, as I set out for my swim. I flinch at the sight of her in the street; grinning, caught with her mouth full. She thrusts an open packet of cheap choc-coated biscuits at me. 'Want a cookie?'

'No thanks.' We've paused on the footpath. Her grin falters. 'I'm not hungry,' I add.

She crunches away, shedding crumbs. 'You don't *look* like you'd eat junk food.'

'I can't eat wheat,' I say. 'I'm allergic to gluten.'

'You're the *healthy* type, that's why you're skinny,' she accuses.

'I'm not healthy,' I say, itching to swim, now, 'just *sensitive*.'

'Have you heard the noise again?' she says.

'Not at all.' It's been more than a fortnight. I smile at her.

'So the Blu-Tack worked!' She looks as if she might be about to give me a high five.

'You've no idea what a relief it is,' I gush. 'You're a treasure, I love you.' And in that moment it's true — at least, compared to how I feel toward Deb.

The triumphant light leaves Stacey's eyes. She turns aside. 'Don't forget' — she's still chewing — 'to come on up and say if my TV's a nuisance.'

And why beholdeſt thou the mote that is in thy brother's eye,
but conſidereſt not the beam that is in thine own eye?

My boyfriend's frying hash browns late one Sunday morning when we hear a loud, jaunty rap. 'Can you get that?' I say from bed. 'Please?'

He sighs and drags his feet to the peephole, reflected in my bedroom mirror. 'It might be your new neighbour,' he reports. 'I've never seen her before.'

'Can you just ask her what it's about?'

A moment later he puts his head in. 'It's Stacey,' is all he'll say.

'Sorry to knock so early,' she blurts when I answer the door, which I hold ajar to conceal my self-portraits as Eve, the Magdalene, the serpent, and more, 'but I was just going to throw this out…unless you wanted it?' She's holding a large box so close to my face that I can't read the label. I back away. 'It's an ice-cream maker.' She beams. 'Good as new.'

'Thanks,' I say, 'but I wouldn't use it, I'm lactose-intolerant,' and as I watch her shoulders droop I think that with all her vacant space, she might be a touch compulsive in her rush to purge what she doesn't want. Our fellow residents dump their junk in the car park across the road. That's where I found one of my shelves and some crockery, I tell her. (That I never find anything useful outside the McMansions in clean-up week accords with my boyfriend's view: the rich aren't all they seem, either.)

She says she'll take it across when the rain stops.

After she's gone my boyfriend says his presence gave her a shock. 'When I saw her through the peephole she looked so pleased with herself, like she was doing something really big, but the second I answered the door she got smaller, sucked it all back in.'

I shrug and, while he scrambles eggs, tell him what I saw yesterday. After my swim I was passing the gate where we'd once heard grunting, when a model-thin platinum blonde emerged from it right in front of me, wearing a black designer ensemble, and as she approached her black BMW I heard more grunts, then saw a small, hairy, black pig in her arms.

My boyfriend nearly burns the buckwheat toast, he laughs so hard.

That which is crooked cannot be made ſtraight :
and that which is wanting, cannot be numbered.

With the six o'clock news droning over my ceiling, I contemplate my Bible's back flyleaf. Did my coeliac gene travel down this maternal line? Did George or Ann, Mary or Joseph, Daniel or Alice have trouble digesting wheat bread? Did any of Great Aunt Ivy's twelve siblings have an S-shaped spine? It could be worse, I remind myself, it's not yet as if I resemble a pretzel; my downstairs neighbour, who's louder than Stacey, could stay at home nights, not just days. Still, I'm trapped in a no-win system. The personal is political. The lesser of two evils is my best hope for peace. Deb nearly bit my head off last time I made an appeal, then ignored it. And I'm at the end of my wits; her telly had been on since lunchtime today, and just when I hear her slam out for the evening, I'm cursed with the babel of Stacey's. I hop out of bed into shoes and a shawl, and pad upstairs during the weather report.

Stacey's face falls when she opens the door. Who was she expecting? An Optus rep? Jehovah's Witnesses? The census collector? Or maybe the return of whoever spent last Monday night in her bed.

'You said to tell you when I could hear it,' I say, filled with guilt at the sight of her frown, 'and it's clear whose it is this time because Deb's gone out.' Stacey's telly, it's clear to me now, isn't all that loud, but maybe the empty space amplifies sounds (the walls are still bare, I notice; I'd have thought she'd use Blu-Tack to hang a few posters), last Monday we heard her, if not her companion, grunting and moaning for hours. And last week I heard her on the phone shouting, 'I haven't done anything *wrong*, Mum!' I hear her cough, stir and chop things, and throw up; hear her flush her toilet most nights, between twelve and dawn, at least once if not twice.

'I'll try turning it down halfway' — she aims the remote — 'and we'll see how that goes.' Her coolness is all the more unsettling because I'm used to her friendly can-do face. But maybe she's just premenstrual; tomorrow's a new moon. 'Thanks so much.' I'm tempted to mention that she and her overnight guest woke us up, but I'm wary of pushing my luck. Besides, the interruption to her solitude seems like a breakthrough. Some days, I've observed, she never goes out, not even to check her mailbox. 'You're sure our TV hasn't bothered you? Or our squabbles? My boyfriend's been stressed —'

'No,' she says in a monotone. 'I don't get any noise from your flat.'

'Really?' I find it hard to believe she's heard none of our yelling about my chronically stiff neck or his ephemeral erections. Come to think of it, we haven't had sex once since she moved in. She shakes her head. I've backed up to the threshold. 'Sorry to bug you,' I say. 'My hearing is sensitive, I took a free test —'

'Your lips look blue,' she says. 'Have you been swimming?'

'Yes,' I say without thinking, though I don't like her tone, 'I wait till the sun goes...'

'It's too cold for swimming.' She sounds so chill, I don't try to explain that it helps ease the headaches from my scoliosis; I just thank her again. 'You're an angel,' I say, and rush off before her glare turns me to stone.

The wind goeth toward the ſouth, and turneth about unto the north; it whirleth about continually, and the wind returneth again according to his circuits.

The next morning after I've waved off my boyfriend, I'm eating gluten-free porridge with soymilk while reading *Jane Eyre* when I hear an almighty slam and feet pounding the stairs. They halt near my door and a howl of rage reaches my ears, but its meaning escapes me, because I'm hearing a voice from the mid-nineteenth century. Not until I've realised Deb's out do the words from the stairwell make sense:

'Can you *please* not come up to my place to complain about my noise ever again!'

Still chewing, I put down my spoon and reread a line four or five times.

'*Bitch!*' screams the voice, and the feet stampede down another flight. '*Bitch!*' it repeats.

I swallow a lump of lukewarm millet and cross the room to gaze out my window. Stacey stands on the lawn below, chin raised toward my balcony, sun at her back. Blood roars in my ears like the ocean. What have I done wrong? I know she can't see me watching, the glass is clouded with windborne salt, but my eyes are sharp for my age and I can see hers bulging out of their sockets, until she storms off up the road, shouting into her mobile.

Unable to face more porridge, I go and sit on my bed. And as I reach for the Bible that's comforted four generations before mine, published in M•DCC•LXXII — before printers ceased to use ſ for s; before this land had seen white settlers; before the invention of television or radio or jumbo jets — I see a pigeon perched on my window ledge, feathers puffed out, neck pulled in. Though normally they swoop off as soon as they glimpse me, roosting as they do along the gutters of the upstairs flat, this bird just blinks as if in sympathy. Lately, rattled by the neighbours, I've been painting less — yet leafing through my Bible more often, imagining it brought peace to those who brought it here, when they came by sea, because it allayed some unspeakable fear; answered some abstract need.

After a while the pigeon takes flight and, recalling neither neighbour is in, I start work on a small blank canvas with unprecedented conviction. Stacey won't be gone long so I want to put the lull to good use.

Yet, that afternoon when a stiff breeze blows in and her with it, and the original squeaking of curtain rods resumes, my new-found concentration barely falters. The sound lacks its old disturbing power now I know the source of it.

Devreaux Baker

Recipe for Lorca's Chocolate Cake

I worked all night on a chocolate cake
for Lorca, filled with light

that does not know what it wants,
created from chocolate so dark it sears hearts

and fills minds with dreams of moon and water.

I used cocoa so pure
it causes policemen to weep.

I filled the layers
with white linen afternoons,

a hint of ginger and essence of rose
creating a dancestep that wakes your spirit

to enter the souls of your feet as a whisper
and fill your body with *duende,*

passion of the first kiss, becoming a river of fire
that ignites your thighs,

and sets loose love reflected in all the eyes of men,
women, children and dogs,

so that one bite of chocolate will rest in your belly
like the tender edge of dawn,

 lifting your voice out of the dark rooms of earth
where you sleep,

rising up like wind or stars to encircle my body

with your words.

Jonathan Greenhaus

From Requena to Iquitos

It's a little before noon
& preadolescents   carefully lay down two-by-fours   into the muck
                       as the riverboat fills up
       at the Amazonian port of Requena.

Friends & families   gather closely   at the division of land & water,
   & enthusiastic lovers   bid passionate farewells
                       on a makeshift muddy pier,
   kissing
as if the world   & all of time & space   were ending,
 as if their own burning lips   would soon disintegrate
                   for lack of continued contact.

Passengers set up rainbow-hued hammocks,
   expertly stringing them
between the deck's endless rows   of cast-iron pillars,   swaying them
                   to check their sturdiness,
   as crowds appear   & disappear
into turns & twists   of suspended fabric.

   As the travelers embark,
pint-sized entrepreneurs pass between their huddled bodies   & sing:
   ¡Hay papel… Hay papel!
Pasta de dientes, cepillo, jaboncillo…   ¡Gaseosa, gaseosa!
                Tapioca…   Tapioca…   Tapioca…
   & they buy these odds — & — ends,
these things they've neglected to bring

while passengers speak   of the fluctuating prices   of banana & watermelon,
   & hatred springs   between rival suitors,
& newborn babies   are cradled   in the devoting arms of young couples.

Amidst all this,
love develops in the furtive glances of strangers   far from loved ones,
                              as they harbor hopes   for a new beginning,
   arriving the next day
at Iquitos' bustling port,   where others impatiently wait at the piers
                                             to replace them
          with the eternal promise   of another departure.

Brennan O'Shea

Don't Wait

Propaganda is a wonderful thing. Some of us ignore it, always. Some of us eventually succumb and adopt 'the right opinion'. Some of us leap onto it with enthusiasm...

My sister Ellie for one: real name Joy, or was it Joyce? We were born on the same day and even at the same time, allegedly, but to different mothers; presumably we had different fathers. I've never bothered to find out, I feel no need to know. I am free to be as I choose without either blaming my forbears or having to give them all the credit.

We were adopted by a couple who liked the idea of having 'disconnected twins' and the chance it gave to prove that astrology is rubbish. They had several birth charts prepared for us by 'reputed' astrologers and bound into books. I keep mine because it's the only thing I have from them: they were killed in a car crash when we were about two and a half.

We grew up by the beach, brought up by Gran, our adopting mother's mother. Gran had either been a teacher or wanted to be one, I forget which, and read to us the stories she called 'classics' and from one of these — the 'Water babes' I think — she took the name Ellie and applied it to my sister who loved both beach and sea so much. My sister loved the name Ellie and always used it from then on, hence my forgetting her original name.

Ellie had long, curly, fair hair — 'golden' Gran called it — and blue eyes and was thought pretty as a child, beautiful as a woman. She was always good natured, obedient, kind...too good to be true, but she was true. She was my sister and everyone loved her.

Those were the days when we were encouraged to respect old people. The local MP's newsletter always pictured him with old people, at a club, or new 'retirement facility' praising their achievements, congratulating those who had lived 100 years, stayed married for 50 years, and so on. Local newspapers had more of the same. The words 'elders' and 'seniors' were almost obligatory, no one dared say, or write, 'old people'. I'm sure there was even a 'senior of the year', a 90 year old who had gained a

Master of Medicine degree, or climbed Everest with a crocodile...Stupid waste of time and effort I thought, but Ellie was full of admiration. She wrote a composition about our wonderful grandmother who looked after us and won the 'Principal's Special Prize' for it, a special prize for she was only ever near top of the lower half of the class. I busted the nose of the only one who dared to say 'dumb blonde' but no matter how hard she worked Ellie was never going to be an English teacher for Gran.

A friend of Gran's took Ellie into her hairdressing business, where she worked even harder and really seemed to have a talent for it. She left to look after Gran, nursing her through Alzheimer's for years, and then cancer. I stayed away, moving around, both here and overseas, as geologists do, and was overseas when Gran died. Ellie sent me a copy of a memoir of Gran that appeared in the local newspaper; the last few lines commended Ellie for her loving care of Gran. It took up two columns of the top half of the page. The third column had part of an article about elders being a drain on the 'social purse', making life harder for the young who had to pay 'crippling taxes' to support 'these people and their expensive health care'.

When I came back, two years later, Ellie had returned to hairdressing. She was still living in Gran's house; fine by me. I like the beach, but prefer the hills and solitary bush walks so I bought an isolated cottage as a base camp, intending to move further out and build my own place when I retired, which I did in my fifties. We lived separate lives, but always met for lunch — 'celebration' was Ellie's word though I didn't see it that way — on our shared birthday.

On the birthday when I reached official retirement age there were two letters in the box; one was a very large envelope, almost certainly the usual effusive card from Ellie, and an official letter:

Your Government commends you for your contribution to society through your past years of employment but regrets that you feel unable to continue in employment. Many citizens find it fulfilling to continue working until their mid-seventies or even longer.

However, it is noted that you have secured adequate financial support and will not be applying for the Government Aid for Elderly Citizens' Allowance [formerly known as Age Pension].

Your Government hopes that you will continue to serve the community in a voluntary capacity.

This letter is to inform you that you must register with GovVolLink for assistance in finding Approved Community Service Employment and to obtain your Community Servant Transport Card which entitles you to free public transport to and from your Approved Community Service Employment.

Your Government is determined to prevent the exploitation of volunteers that has occurred in the past and, in particular, to ensure that all Occupational Health and Safety regulations are complied with so it is now illegal to undertake any Community Service Employment without GovVolLink approval. If you have commenced working in any sort of voluntary capacity you must register with GovVolLink within 2 weeks of receiving this letter.

Your Government wishes you the best of health.

Unfortunately some older Citizens suffer from extremely painful and debilitating problems so, in the cause of alleviating human misery Your Government has arranged for all Senior Citizens to receive the Government Compassion Package. This should arrive within 2 weeks of this letter. Should this not occur, please contact my department.

Jocelyn Smith
Seniors Consultant Specialist
Ministry of Human Services

Sod that for a lark! I thought. What kind of no-hoper has to work for nothing? Besides, I've earned my retirement and I intend to enjoy it. I threw the letter into the bin.

One of the small pleasures of retirement is getting up when one wakes, no more bullying by an alarm clock, and I was at risk of being late. That day was bright and sunny, warm for the time of year, perfect for lunch by the beach, but it was an hour's drive to get to Kafe Athene, Ellie's favourite place.

Every station I tuned to seemed to have a talk back program with someone complaining about the high taxes we paid because so much was spent on the 'selfish oldies'…definitely not what I wanted to hear. Finally I found a station playing the most extraordinary jazz version of Beethoven's fifth that I have ever heard. It was one of those volunteer-run community stations and I was about to ring them for details of the CD. when I noticed that I was right behind a police car.

As I said, I'd earned my retirement and I meant to enjoy it. And I did, building my own house and travelling. Mostly overseas but back here in later years when the 'be-patriotic-and-holiday-at-home' advertisements had ceased; and, to be truthful, I was tired of long flights. After the last such trip I spent two weeks eating and sleeping and sorting through mail, throwing ninety percent of it away. Another official letter, about six months old, was there:

This letter is to inform you that legislation is now in force requiring all citizens over the age of 17 and not in paid employment to contribute a minimum of 2 years Approved Community Service Employment to society.

According to GovVolLink records you have not taken part in any Approved Community Service Employment.

As you reached age 70 just before legislation was passed you are exempt but Your Government would like to encourage you to take part in Service to the Community. You will surely find it most fulfilling, as so many other Citizens have, and a great way to enjoy the company of your fellow Citizens.

Please be aware that any sort of voluntary work, even looking after sick or disabled family members must be registered with GovVolLink for assessment as Approved Community Service Employment.

Your Government gives formal acknowledgement to contributing Citizens by funding Local Government Community Service Employment morning tea ceremonies at which Volunteer of the Year certificates in various categories are awarded.

Please note that the Government Compassion Package sent to you 5 years ago has been superseded.

Your updated Government Compassion Package will be sent to you in the next 2 weeks. Should this not occur, please contact me at the address/phone number/email address at the top of this letter.

Your GP can assist you if you have any difficulty understanding the instructions.

Jocelyn Smith
Seniors Consultant Specialist
Ministry of Human Services

No sign of any package in the pile of mail; perhaps because no one was there to sign for it. I had not seen Ellie for a couple of years; I wondered what effect that letter had had on her. Deliberately, I had not contacted her for our recent birthday 'celebration'; I regretted that now. She had been working at two jobs when I left, anxious not to be a burden on the young, determined to look after herself.

'I'm going to do what it says in the National Seniors' Advice. It's from the government, not a paper or magazine or on television so don't tell me it's all rubbish!' she had said. She stopped short of telling me how selfish I am.

We agreed to meet for lunch the next day, not at Kafe Athene, but at a pub some streets away and not overlooking the beach. It was a pub that offered 'pensioner' meals; nothing fancy but reasonable quality at a reasonable price in a clean, light dining room, handy for the 'pokies'. It was close to one of the three High Level Care facilities where she now worked as a volunteer. One of her employers had sacked her because she looked old — 'not a good advertisement for the salon' — and when a friend showed her an article about 'selfish oldies' keeping young people out of paid work by 'hanging on' too long Ellie had decided to leave the other job. She sold Gran's house and invested the money as advised by a government financial advisor so that she had an income and even though she qualified she had managed, so far, not to apply for the Government Aid for Elderly Citizens.

'I'm so happy. It really is fulfilling you know!' and she did, indeed, look happy; if tired. Not old though; Ellie always looked young. Too late to challenge the sacking now, even if she would let me. I felt angry, but managed to say nothing.

'I have a late birthday present for you.' She gave me a suitcase containing things from Gran's house that she thought I might like to have.

Congratulations on being one of the first recipients of the new GovCares Kit. This replaces the former Australian Government Compassion Package.

If you have any difficulty at all in understanding the instructions you should contact your GP, who, thanks to recently passed amendments to Equal Opportunity legislation, is legally obliged to assist you in the use of the GovCares Kit.

Alternatively, as you are now 75, you can access assistance and counselling from the newly established Assistance to Venerable Australians

wing of the Department of Human Services.
Argyle Zatopek
Minister for Human Services

That one was waiting for me when I came back from a two year long camping trip on which, deliberately, I had kept away even from very small towns. My success in being self-sufficient while travelling was gratifying, now I intended to live that way at home. I hoped Ellie would join me. I began work on a speech, something about ending our lives together as we had begun them. Sickening, but only sentimental slush like that would have a chance of persuading her.

The next day's mail had an invitation to 'The Shining Example'. The State Governor, Federal Government Ministers, the State Premier, and various others would be in attendance; and my sister would be in the leading role. For the first time in her life.

I know I should have been there too, but I couldn't, I just couldn't support what she was doing.

I went back to the pub where we'd last met for lunch. It had changed, as things do, as things should. The dining room had become a sort of local sports museum: photos, trophies, records of scores in games over twenty years and suchlike had replaced the rural prints and vases of flowers. There were even more TV screens showing different sports programs. I looked around, glancing at the staff: they all seemed to be new, no one to recognize me. My guess that the corner screen would still show 'national interest' news items was correct. I bought a beer, took it to a table in a corner where the screen could be viewed without, I hoped, anyone viewing me. I couldn't hear everything too well because of the general noise level in the bar but that didn't matter, I didn't want to hear all the political speeches; I really didn't want to hear my sister. I feared I would succumb to reading the captions. I was right about that.

First, of course, the National Anthem, then speeches, all praising the 'unavoidably absent' Argyle Zatopek, the architect of the scheme, for his foresight: such ingenuity and such humanity. Of course! No such person — a commitee. Has to be. 'He' was next praised for his brilliance in composing the scheme's anthem:

'Don't wait to be told
You don't need to grow old'

Then sung by a choir — almost — but cut off for advertisements. The program came back just in time for the procession.

So there she was, in a long, flowing, white robe with her long flowing, white hair floating out behind her as she walked — floated almost — along a white carpet. She carried a bunch of white lilies, holding it, very tightly, with both hands. The reporter said she looked 'angelic' — I bet that was scripted for him — and described the expression on her face as 'seraphic'. I'd have said 'soppy'. He went on about 'the vision in white leading the procession'. She was followed by three groups of relatives, looking grim, some weeping, and each carrying a picture of one of the 'examples' from the High Level Care Facilities where Ellie worked. Every 'example' was inspired by Ellie according to the commentator.

That, I could understand. In such a state of health, having to endure life in such places, why not? Next was a shot of the 'examples': all in white, each with a lily, and with an attendant standing by. Only Ellie had been alone.

The program was interrupted for an important horse race. A caption said they would come back to it but I felt sick already. I left. I walked along the street wondering how such a shy nervous person as my sister could be part of such a show. It occurred to me later that she might have been drugged. I hope she was.

There are pictures of Ellie in every suburb or small town now. She has become a sort of saint: there are 'Shining Example' ceremonies every month and a special one commemorating her every year, on our birthday. I avoid them.

I'm 93 today. No letter from the government this time. They can't find me. I'm sure of that. I'm a permanent camper now and probably the oldest person in the country. It can't last of course. Not that I want to make the ton, but I am determined to die of natural causes.

And to hell with their blasted GovCares Kit.

Jeffery Alfier

After Barkeep Angelique Closes at *Pequod Tavern*

Out in the parking lot under the weak
light of a waxing moon, I count
the tattoos that strut up her arm.
Eight green ones, all Chinese dragons.

A single red one is inscribed like a bloody
harpoon against Melville's imperilled
sea. And there's one more, just north
of her pubic bone. Or so the rumors go.

She tracks my eyes sliding up her arm,
swears she got them in the Marquesas
Islands, and pulls out a hash pipe
tucked somewhere below her belt.

The herb is brown or blond, the best
Morocco offers. Her deep-winter eyes
shine in streetlight, and I come to know
they'd subdue the heart of any feral beast.

As our shared smoke sinks in, my head
clouds with chimeras. She says most
nights it's the hoodoo of this sweet smoke
that keeps the demons at bay. Other nights

it's the switchblade tucked in her bra,
veiled from the commerce of bourbon
and sweat. She wonders if the blade
is worth more than the blood it could take.

Richard King Perkins II

Carl the Mechanic

Carl the mechanic
was the first poet
I ever met —
livin' at home
takin' a few classes
at the local college
I think us younger guys
in the neighborhood
kinda looked up to him
because he was sort
of a regular guy
but when he
came out cryin' one day
and showed us his
first publication
he sniffed that he'd
tried to show
his old man
what he'd done
and all the old drunk
could do was laugh
and drip snot
all over the pages
Carl said this was typical
of how people
treated poets
which was why I knew
I'd never be one
so I asked Carl
to pop the hood
of the Charger
and show me
the spark plugs
or something.

Tobi Cogswell

Miss Lydia's Dance School and Social Club

Only blue house on the block
with graveled lawn for overflow
from neat curbs, addresses painted
with the American Flag in front,
a 5 dollar donation to a worthwhile
charity collected from and agreed upon
by all the neighbors, drunk or sober.

He left Miss Lydia with just the couch —
the rest of the downstairs spent to pay
off debts as he was running from a good
life to nowhere fast. Miss Lydia
mirrored the living room. Monday through
Thursday, town mothers sat on the couch,
watched their gawky daughters pose and preen.

On Friday nights Miss Lydia wrestled
ancient folding tables and yard-sale chairs.
Careful not to pinch herself she pushed
the couch against a mirrored wall,
got ready for cards. Admission
was a fifth of something hard and a pocket
of quarters. Miss Lydia bought mixers.

If gentlemen brought a liqueur they could stay
the night, fall asleep, the sweetly licoriced
whispers of Miss Lydia on their smile.
They all took turns bringing Sambuca
or Amaretto — never the same thing, never
the same Friday. Mornings meant poached
eggs, put away the tables and head on home,

their leftover winnings on the kitchen
counter — a donation for next Friday
when tablecloths would be white as the
panties just explored, smelling just
as sweet, their man-calendars marked
for when they could explore, once more,
the graceful and creative Miss Lydia.

Kenneth Hudson

The Poet's Eye

for Andrew Burke

My friend has a camera embedded in his head.
Sensations are the lens.
Perceptions are the rest.
Everything's recorded in a constant flow
later edited into poems.

Like a painter learns not to see forms
but the negative space that surrounds
their outlines   silhouettes them.
This demands natural ability
and decades of hard practice.
A 'poet's eye' doesn't come easily.

But he's done it for so long
it's now automatic and unconscious
so everything he writes
has become one continuous poem.

Fikret Pajalic

Oreo

The more one comes to know men,
the more one comes to admire the dog.
Joussenel

Oreo watched through the window of a sixth floor flat. The view was breathtaking. It extended from the dark mountain range on the right, across the green, yellow and red flatlands and all the way to the blue sea on the left. In rare moments when there was quiet Oreo learnt to appreciate the beauty of the vast landscape. In the distance tiny boats and huge ships dotted the shimmering surface of the ocean. At times a flock of white birds would fly by on their way to the sea. As they passed her window they squawked 'hello' to her. She envied their freedom.

Oreo shared the flat with the man with dark sideburns, a thin woman with long fingernails and their son who always wore a hat. The man and the woman had lots of drawings on their skin. A small white stick with a flame at the end was always in their mouths or hands.

Oreo came to live with this family one rainy day, a little before her first birthday. The boy with the hat came to the house where she lived with her mother. Their master gave away all Oreo's siblings, five in number, over the previous months. Oreo knew that one day she would be gone too. She had mixed feelings about it. She was sad to leave her mother, but happy to leave master who was always angry and treated them badly.

Master and Hat-Boy spoke in loud voices. Hat-Boy said he didn't want a bitch. Master replied that 'bitches were as ferocious as males, you've just got to train them right.' Hat-Boy was promised a male and he wasn't going to pay top dollar for a female.

'I'm a hundred bucks short; it's all I got.' He firmly stuck out his hand full of cash in front of Master's face.

Master, who could smell the crumpled notes, contemplated the situation for an instant. He was close to kicking out the youngster back on the street where he belonged with the other riff-raff, but the bitch he wanted to sell showed no promise, too scrawny for breeding and too timid for fights. He hated how she tried to get pats out of him. The last one of the litter to be sold was always an average dog at best, he reckoned.

'Bullshit,' Master raised his voice just enough to scare the boy but not to chase him away. He snatched the money from his hand. 'Just this time and never again, you hear me mate? You better not say one fucking word to anyone or I will never sell you another dog.'

Hat-Boy hurriedly put Oreo in the box with holes on the side and tucked it under his arm.

When he was at the door Master yelled after him: 'You're getting a bloody pit bull for peanuts, mate.'

Hat-Boy ran to his car. The rain was beating down hard now. Inside he lifted the sides of the box and dropped in some dried dog food. While Oreo was eating he spoke to her.

'That breeder prick didn't tell me your name.'

Oreo barked twice, not too loud and not too forceful, just enough to acknowledge her new master and present herself as friendly. She hoped for the best and the boy seemed pleasant.

Hat-Boy watched his new dog eat. Oreo was a stocky dog with stumpy legs and no neck. She had a short coat, which was all white except a splash of black on her back and belly. Hat-Boy put one hand in the box, petted her head and scratched her withers.

'Oreo,' he exclaimed, 'I'll call you Oreo.'

As he walked into the flat, Hat-Boy slammed the door to announce his return. Water ran off his jacket and dripped onto the dirty carpet. His parents were in front of the television. The loud bang of the door brought his father back to reality but his mother stayed in Zombieland. Oreo was at Hat-Boy's side, leashed with a short piece of greasy tie-down rope. It sat tight on her neck chafing her skin. She struggled to breathe.

Hat-Boy's father slowly peeled his eyes off the screen and looked at his son. He brought the can of beer to his mouth, took a lengthy swig and then wiped his lips with the bottom of his singlet. Hat-Boy's mother was motionless, her head on the armrest. Hair covered her face and her shirt was wet on her chest.

'Who is your girlfriend, mate?' Sideburns-Man asked, his lips stretched into a grin showing his cigarette-stained dentures.

'Oreo, she's my new...' Hat-Boy started excited, but his father interrupted him with a scoff.

'Fuck me, mate. You couldn't give a pit bull a sweeter name, huh?' He hit his temple with his forefinger and shook his head in disapproval. 'And why the fuck did you get a bitch?' Sideburns-Man continued. 'Can't you see we have enough of them?' He shoved his wife with his foot and her limp body slumped onto the floor.

Sideburns-Man stood and revealed a large wet patch on his crotch. With the small careful steps of a drunkard he approached Oreo. His unsteady hand went down to grab her by the neck, but she hid behind Hat-Boy's legs.

Sideburns-Man straightened up, pinched his son's left cheek and gave it a patronising slap. 'She's no fighter, mate.' He brought his face right up to his son's. The foul smell of beer and urine overpowered Hat-Boy and he screwed up his face in disgust.

'You'll make this much dough from her.' He made a circle with his thumb and forefinger and planted it on his son's forehead. He then pointed at Oreo, belched and said, 'Just a dog, that's all.'

Sunny days replaced the rainy ones. Different kinds of birds were in the air. Oreo watched through the window down onto the street. People walking on the sidewalk looked small and not scary. They walked fast never looking up. Only the birds knew of her existence.

Hat-Boy took her on a drive to the countryside. When paddocks, trees and farms replaced the concrete, Oreo thought that he was taking her back to Master. Instead he took her to a large isolated warehouse where there was a gathering of dogs and people. There she met other dogs that looked like her and people approached her, but never in a friendly way. They lifted her ears, checked her paws, pried open her jaw and looked under her tail.

Hat-Boy held her on a short leash and lifted her off the ground so her front legs dangled in the air while she gasped for air. She was exposed to all the touches and probes and she hated being vulnerable.

Some of the men said things like 'not bad' and 'she's got potential' during this. Most stayed silent, non-committal. She was afraid of the other dogs but she discerned that she must put on her bravest face and for the most part she blended in.

Oreo sensed by the way Hat-Boy was tugging on her leash and taking her from one side of the warehouse to the other that he was getting angry, impatient. He had a heated conversation with two men at the main door and after a fair bit of talking he was told 'no money, no fight' and shown the door.

That night Hat-Boy taped kitchen towels to his forearms and he put on two pairs of long welding gloves, panting and swearing as he did it. During the battle with the gloves his hat fell off and his shaved skull was uncovered. There was a red mark around his head from the rim of his hat.

When he was done he ordered Oreo to bite him. She stayed still. Over the next few minutes Hat-Boy got progressively more agitated by Oreo's unwillingness to cooperate. He smacked her on her ears and pulled her teats really hard until the pain got the better of her and she retaliated by biting.

She was very careful and never bit too hard. With the utmost self-control she managed to keep in check her most natural tendency. Her powerful jaws locked onto the loose part at the end of the glove near the elbow. The blood inside her veins got hot and muscles she didn't know she had came alive. Her whole body became taut like a loaded spring and it seemed that things around her slowed down a fraction. Just enough for her to anticipate Hat-Boy's every move.

She hung off the glove like her ancestors once hung off bulls' noses until their tenaciousness and unstoppable strength brought the rampaging bulls down, slowly suffocating them. She became aware of who she really was and of her purpose. It was humans who made her, and others like her, into killers.

But she would never hurt the boy that way. Hat-Boy was her new master, an inept one, but a master nonetheless. She learnt from her old one that a master's anger should not be tested, as often pain would follow.

She expected punishment for her transgression, but the boy seemed curiously satisfied with her efforts and this confused Oreo.

Hat-Boy's father walked into the bedroom while Oreo slept in the corner. She was already awake, but the boy was snoring as if he had a toy tractor stuck in his throat. Sideburns-Man kicked the bed and shouted at the boy to 'get the fuck up.' Under the blanket the boy growled at him to 'fuck off.'

'Did you bloody forget about school?' Sideburns-Man said as he pulled a cigarette from a packet on the floor and stuck it between his teeth.

Hat-Boy got up slowly, rubbing his face like he was kneading dough. His head was heavy and hurting. He was annoyed that his old man, in rare moments of lucidity, actually remembered some stuff from everyday life. Like groceries, showering, school.

As Hat-Boy left the flat with a piece of stale bread in his mouth, he asked his father to feed Oreo while he was out. Normally he would ask a favour from his mother, who was a touch more reliable, but she was gone already. It was her Monday morning religious trip to the 'Church of Pokies'. She would save up most of the dole money that she received every second Thursday and went to play the slots on Monday mornings.

'The place is bloody empty until midday,' she reasoned. 'No dickheads around that I have to listen to.'

Hat-Boy didn't understand. He went one time with her to the club and as soon as she walked inside her 'temple' nothing else existed for her. She only opened her mouth for another drag on her cigarette.

He was running to catch a bus and tried to recall if he fed Oreo last night. Playing video games, watching television and smoking weed that he stole from his mother's handbag, he remembered. The weed was awful, the worst grade he ever smoked. It gave him a pounding headache before knocking him out. He figured that if the dog didn't complain during the night he must have given her food, so he hopped on the bus.

But Oreo did complain. She jumped on the bed and tried to wake Hat-Boy by sticking her muzzle into his face and gently nudging his head. She licked his face, pulled his sleeves, sat on his stomach, made small whining noises that eventually built up to a growl and when nothing else worked, she barked.

First quietly, a couple of short woofs. Soon her barks increased to a sustained crescendo, but no one in the flat could hear her. At last she barked not just because she was hungry, but because she was scared that something had happened to her master, Hat-Boy. She only stopped after an angry neighbour thumped on the wall screaming obscenities.

Sideburns-Man had a glint of hatred in his eyes. Oreo watched his lips move. 'Dumb dog,' he said and closed the door behind her. She didn't trust him.

By mid-morning Sideburns-Man was on his fourth beer. Oreo's stomach was twisting and her tongue was hanging out of her mouth. She jumped on the windowsill and tried to ignore it. Two turtledoves landed on the roof opposite and groomed themselves. They helped her forget hunger for a few short moments. Soon the weakness overcame her body and she started howling in pain. Hat-Boy would hear this, she was sure.

It was Sideburns-Man who heard it. Annoyed, he ran into the room and rushed toward Oreo. Instinctively her brain reacted, she leapt on the bed, assumed her defensive stance and growled showing her fangs. Sideburns-Man tried to hit her, but Oreo snapped her jaws, saliva flew off her jowls showering him, narrowly missing his hand. He backed off instantly.

'There is some bloody pit bull in you after all,' Sideburns-Man said taken aback. He lifted his forefinger threateningly, but did nothing.

He walked outside the flat and knocked on the neighbour's door. A small man, shriveled like a prune, wearing only underpants opened the door.

'Oh, we came to apologise, finally,' the neighbour snorted at Sideburns-Man.

'What fucking for?'

'For your fucking dog who barked all fucking night and woke up the whole fucking building.'

Sideburns-Man cocked his head to the side, not understanding what the man was talking about. He considered smacking the skinny prick right in his noggin but changed his mind fast.

'Oh, that. Yes.' He pretended. 'That's why I'm here. I need to borrow your son's cricket bat. I'm going to teach that bitch a lesson in proper behavior.'

'Your wife's beyond help, mate. I'd say it's time to kick her to the curb,' the neighbour said with a self-satisfying grin on his face, pleased with his wittiness. His chicken chest produced a whizzing sound while he snickered at his own joke.

Sideburns-Man took a deep breath. He was in disbelief that he didn't react to this insult. First the bat, then the dog, then I'll come after you, you ugly cunt, he thought. With great effort he cracked a fake smile.

'Funny, funny. The bat, please?' He mustered some politeness.

'Down the hall, second bedroom on right, under the bed,' the instructions came. 'And don't get blood on it, all right?'

Sideburns-Man returned to his flat and a long, high-pitched, uninterrupted whining greeted his ears. He felt as if someone was putting his brain through a slicing machine. With the bat in hand he ran toward the door but stopped himself when he touched the doorknob. She's a pit bull and there's no fucking with them. He knew exactly what damage they could do.

The only thing he took away from numerous visits to dogfights that cost him a fortune was an appreciation of the ferocity of a pit bull. Still amazed that men could turn such innocent-looking pups into brutal killers, he recognised he needed a plan. He made sure the door to his son's room was locked, and then left the flat. Grog was on his mind and time on his side.

Mid-afternoon he returned carrying a near empty bottle of the cheapest whiskey he could find in one hand and a bag in the other. The strong liquor took the dampness out of his bones and he felt bulletproof. Sideburns-Man was ready for Oreo. He put the bottle on the table, pulled a fishing net out of the bag and took the cricket bat that was leaning on the wall.

Oreo was stretched out on the bed staring at the ceiling. Her mind wandered to the days when she huddled between the warm bodies of her siblings, all eagerly sucking on her mother's teats. She missed her mother's gentle licks on her face. Even her mother's rebuke she remembered fondly, usually with her front paw, or if she was really naughty with a quick bite on her neck.

When her eye noticed a fast moving mass coming toward her, she barely had time to stand on her feet, lift her head and assess the situation. Next she saw something fall over her from above. Sideburns-Man came into her vision. He was carrying a club, a tool of punishment.

She tried to jump off the bed, but her legs got tangled in the holes of the material that covered her whole body. The more she tried to free herself, the more trapped she became. Very quickly she was unable to move. Barking and growling presented a problem as the thin nylon of the fishing net cut around her neck and face. She was subdued without a fight.

Sideburns-Man pulled her off the bed and she fell on the floor with a thump. He stood over her and kicked her in the ribs and she could see his mouth opening, but she could not hear him. His wild eyes were dancing left and right. The next moment she felt a great blow of the club across her belly. Empty of air, her lungs burned. Another blow followed and she passed out.

Sideburns-Man kicked Oreo's limp body with his foot. The cricket bat was still in his hands, ready to hit her again. When he was sure that she was out he sat on the bed and lit a cigarette. He drew on the cigarette and observed it while it smoldered between his fingers. When he was almost finished he knelt down and put it out on Oreo's neck. She was unmoving while her flesh and fur burnt.

Oreo started coming back to her senses. While she gasped and growled a conclusion formed in Sideburns-Man's mind. He walked to the window, opened it, picked up Oreo, and threw her out.

The vet nurse at the reception desk was on the phone when she heard a screech of tyres. She looked up and watched as the Post Office van turned into the clinic car park and came to an abrupt halt in front of the door. The postman lifted a bundle from the passenger seat and ran into the clinic. In his arms lay a mangled dog covered in fishing net and wrapped in his jacket.

'Please hurry, the dog's still alive,' he pleaded.

The vet nurse opened the swinging door and ushered him in to the hallway behind her. As the Postman walked down the darkened hall and toward the operating room, he left a trail of blood behind him.

The sharp acrid odour with a hint of something rotten that permeated the whole building, started giving the vet a migraine a couple of years ago. There was no point getting upset about it, she would endure another couple of years and retire.

The same was true of her hair. Long curls of strawberry blonde, she was once so proud of, now limp white strands that looked like someone had pasted them on her skull, if she didn't put them in a bun. She had to wash her hair daily as the smell clung to it and she would not get a respite otherwise.

The only way to get rid of the smell of animals' blood, urine, excrement, medication and food would be to dip the whole clinic in a giant bucket filled with industrial strength bleach, she fantasized. White

Hair-Woman knew that she would take 'the kennel smell' to her grave. That's where a stench like this belongs. That's where Oreo belonged. Buried beneath earth and in peace.

White Hair-Woman moved through the hallways, past the consultation and operating rooms to the back of the clinic where the smell was less prominent. She reached the therapy and rehabilitation section of the building and approached room eighteen.

She picked up the chart from the holder on the door and walked in. Oreo lay in the corner of the room chained to the floor. White Hair-Woman sat on the chair in the opposite corner. Regardless of the bitter argument she had with her daughter last night she knew what she had to do.

'There must be something that can be done,' her child insisted full of youthful belief in good triumphing over evil.

She bit her lower lip as her daughter talked and she drifted off. Her decision had been made weeks ago and now she had to play the part of judge and executioner. This was not what she signed up for when she decided to become a Vet.

In the preceding months White Hair-Woman watched as Oreo slowly recovered from her horrific physical injuries. Her chart read like a horror movie script: all legs fractured, severe ligament damage, shattered ribs, bruised lungs, liver injury, internal bleeding, cigarette burns on the skin.

Since she'd operated on Oreo, she observed her every day. She watched her during the first rehabilitation sessions when Oreo just sat in the corner wanting to be left alone. Like today, like everyday. When Oreo bit her first handler and took a chunk off the calf of the second one, when a behavioural specialist tried in vain for a whole week to engage Oreo and when the dog just stayed oblivious to everything, White Hair-Woman was there.

Over time she witnessed Oreo becoming increasingly agitated when people were around and handling her. She displayed aggression toward other dogs in the shelter and went out of her way to pick a fight, targeting dogs twice her size.

All of this suffering could have ended if only she was on duty when Oreo was brought to the clinic. The owner of the dog threw Oreo out of a sixth floor flat while intoxicated. She fell on top of the Postman's van. The conscientious Postman scraped the dog from the roof of his van and brought her to the clinic on White Hair-Woman's day off.

One of her assistants, a young girl full of passion, like her daughter, 'worked' on the dog. The young vet managed to bring the dog back from the dead and stabilize her, then she called White Hair-Woman at home. The words 'urgent' and 'horrific injuries' came from the receiver. Her experience was needed in the operating room, she was told.

She rushed to the clinic, got prepped, read the chart and her grandfather came into her mind, a man who survived two wars. She must have been ten or eleven when one lazy afternoon they rode their bikes into the heart of their family orchard and ate apples, pears, plums, apricots and peaches until they couldn't move. Her grandfather was in a good mood and wore a short-sleeved shirt. On his forearm was a faded tattoo, six digits that she knew about from her parents and other relatives.

She wanted to hear from him about the camps and the chambers and the wires and the tattoo and the loss. She needed to know and she asked him. Her grandfather lifted his hand to cover his eyes from the late summer sun that sat low on the horizon. He opened his mouth, took a deep breath, one of those people take when they're about to tell a story, and he sat there for a moment not breathing. But all he said was, 'for some things, darling, there are no words.'

Years later when she saw Oreo that sentence finally made sense. She understood that for true evil that existed in the world there are no appropriate words. To believe it, one must experience it, like her grandfather did, or see it like she did.

White Hair-Woman watched Oreo for the full hour of her lunch break. The dog never moved. It seemed to her that Oreo knew that she would never have peace again. A private citizen could not adopt Oreo and dog sanctuaries with a 'no kill' policy were not prepared to take her in. Her behaviour problems would require her to be kept in isolation for the remainder of her life. Locked up. Alone.

White Hair-Woman pulled a zip-lock bag from her side-pocket and emptied it. Dog treats laced with sedative dropped to the ground. Oreo lifted her eyes briefly and her nostrils widened, before returning to her position. White Hair-Woman picked up the chart and wrote a word in the recommendation section.

'Sorry that it took me so long,' she said to Oreo and walked out.

When she returned an hour later she found dog asleep. Oreo's paws twitched and her jaws were biting the air.

Oreo was dreaming her last dream. It was a dream that awoke the primordial instincts encoded deep in her DNA. A dream unlike any other took her to a place far away and a time long ago.

On a snowy meadow surrounded with fir trees, a lone white and black bulldog was trying to overcome a large bull. A man with a floppy hat with three points played the lute and danced around a jeering crowd. The bull was tied to an iron stake and could not move more than thirty paces. His nose was blown full of pepper to enrage the animal before the spectacle. The bull was as black as the darkest night and his white horns were smeared with blood. Against the white snow he stood tall and bloody as the beast that haunted the dreams of the villagers. Around him there lay half a dozen lifeless dogs, gored, maimed and trampled.

The bulldog attacked the exhausted bull from behind, but the bull kept distance between them by wildly kicking his hind legs. On several occasions the bulldog barely escaped his hoofs.

After having no success with his approach, the bulldog decided on another tactic. He charged the bull from the front and aimed for his neck, but mistimed the leap and his jaws locked on the bull's nostrils. The bull produced terrible bellows filled with pain. He shook his head from side to side. The bulldog flew through the air but his stocky body remained firmly attached to his prey's face.

Neither beast gave up. The bulldog realised that he lacked bulk to bring the bull down so he unclenched his jaws. The bull fell to the ground exhausted while the bulldog ran to a molehill nearby and hungrily swallowed the spongy earth. The bulldog knew he could vomit this later when he was done with the bull. The mob watched in disbelief.

Now a few kilograms heavier the bulldog charged again. The bull managed to pull the stake out of the frozen ground and began fleeing. He ran as fast as his beaten body would allow toward the edge of the forest. But the bulldog was invigorated with his new plan and with victory in sight. He was on the bull in a flash. The bulldog ran across the bull's back and locked his mighty jaws under his neck. The bull lifted his head in the air as the bulldog hung off his dewlap. His eyes rolled as he let out a thunderous bellow of defeat. The bull fell to the ground.

The snow turned red.

Oreo woke up lying on her back, strapped to a cold stainless steel table with two fluorescent lights piercing her eyes from above. The bull's bellows of pain still thundered in her head.

Hat-Boy waited until 4 am. The only thing he could hear from the living room was the monotonous snoring coming from his father's mouth. He walked to the main bedroom and found his mother sound asleep. On the sofa in the living room his father was making grunting noises. He pulled the middle cushion from behind him. Not looking at his face, he covered it with a cushion and sat on it.

His father's arms flapped around for a little while. He felt his chest rise a few times and then it seemed that his lungs just caved in. The short struggle surprised him. Beer and weed did half the job for him. He picked up the TV remote control from the armrest and flicked the channels until he saw wolves running on the screen.

'A wolf pack is a hierarchical unit. Wolves have established a highly organised and functional society, which is their strength. As Kipling famously said: "For the strength of the Pack is the Wolf, and the strength of the Wolf is the Pack,"' the voice from the box said in a drone and Hat-Boy put the remote back on the armrest.

He moved the cushion underneath him to get more comfortable.

White Hair-Woman's emotional detachment, necessary for her professional survival, started with a wild rabbit infected with myxi. Poor bunny, considered a pest by many, was found in someone's backyard, covered in lumps, shivering in blindness. The rabbit was dumped in front of the clinic's door, left in a box. It was always a box, unless a dog, then a leash to the nearest post.

White Hair-Woman remembered finding a seagull in a box. His limp head was moving uncontrollably from left to right, a sign of blunt object trauma, most likely from flying into a building after being chased by bird of prey. Before she even opened the door she snapped its neck. She found herself despising dumpers.

Years of practice taught her that removing herself from suffering is the only way to cope. Still, it surprised her when it happened, like discovering the first white hair on your scalp or the hint of crow's feet under your eyes. Now that emotional detachment was part of her, there was no going back.

The vet nurse who prepped Oreo left only one syringe on the table for her. They called it 'the second needle', an inappropriate name for a device that delivers death.

There was no need for the first needle that renders the animal unconscious. There were no owners who wished to say their last goodbye before the second needle. No sobbing children hugging their limp furry friends. No one to say goodbye to Oreo.

Putting down a pit bull wasn't a novelty for her, she had euthanised half a dozen. All were deemed too dangerous for society. These dogs had attacked or bitten a person and in one awful case a toddler was mauled to death. In every case the animal was put down while the human walked away with a fine. On one occasion a pit bull was left in front of the door, bitten, scratched and bleeding, cowering in terror, the victim of dog fighting. The unspeakable things humans were capable of, to create a beast for the sole purpose of killing and then blame the beast for its savagery.

She stood above Oreo whose eyes were closed. Her chest was rising up and down rhythmically. White Hair-Woman leaned over and her shadow covered dog's face and Oreo opened her eyes still squinting because of the strong light. She moved the bulbs away and Oreo recognised the human with the ball of white hair on her head.

White Hair-Woman looked Oreo straight in her eyes. Anger and pain swirled in the two brown pools that seemed to take everything in. Like a black hole, there was no escaping the torment that came out of her pupils.

For a moment White Hair-Woman couldn't breathe properly. It was as if the look of suffering drew all the air out her lungs. The feeling of the pointlessness of life, that she'd felt early in her career when putting down animals, returned unexpectedly. She felt weakness in her knees and heaviness in her arms. Oreo barked shaking her out of stupor. White Hair-Woman saw Oreo staring at her.

She placed the needle on Oreo's chest and quickly found the vein. The hollow needle pierced the dog's tough skin. She looked at the dog's face again, but this time Oreo avoided her eyes.

She pressed the needle a little further in until it sat firmly. Thumb pushed the plunger into the barrel and pentobarbital rushed into Oreo's bloodstream. Oreo scrunched her eyes and clenched her jaws. After little time her mouth parted and her lungs took their last breath. White and black body relaxed and her paws dropped. Oreo exhaled for the last time.

Oreo kept her eyes fixated on White Hair-Woman with a syringe in her hand. She noticed how the woman's face paled to white and how indecisiveness shook her hands. She could not let this human fail her. She barked and this shook the doctor out of her haze. Oreo lifted her head and looked inside her soul. The stare chased away White Hair-Woman's doubt. The struggle that commenced the moment Oreo was born was nearing the end. This life is no life.

Oreo felt the small stab in her chest and her mind quickly got cloudy. Her rib cage constricted and body stiffened. She let out her last breath and she was weightless. Nothingness enveloped her.

Oreo was free.

Dedicated to the real Oreo, may she rest in peace and love.

Mark Konik

From a Great Height

Character: Dan – A twenty-seven year old accountant.
Setting: A meeting room in a high rise office in an important city.
Time: Current year, the play takes place in the afternoon.

The stage is set with a chair in the middle. Enter DAN from the side of the stage, dressed in a business suit and tie. He walks quickly onto the stage and is visibly happy and pleased with himself. When he comes near the chair he jumps onto it and faces the audience.

DAN

She said yes, she didn't say no, she said yes. I looked her dead straight in the eye and I asked her. I had no nervous cough, no itchy eyes. Confident, I oozed cool, well for at least a couple of seconds. I was the brave lion showing off his mane to woo the lioness into his den. *(As if he is talking to someone)* Beth, would you like to come to dinner and a show on Friday night? I've been able to get some fantastic seats. My voice didn't waver and I didn't get the squeak I sometimes get in my voice. My body language was good. I talked with my hands, but not too much of course, just the right amount. I thought I was Napoleon when he was conquering Europe; I strutted on in as if I owned the world. I was brave and looked stoic in victory. I had my grin *(DAN shows off his grin)*. I think that was what sealed it, the grin. It was monumental; they should erect a statue of me with my grin. And she said yes straight away. It was like she was waiting for me to ask. Her answer was yes. I still can't believe it, she actually said yes. She didn't even think about it. It was spontaneous, totally spontaneous.

(DAN pauses for a moment.)

She didn't even really think about it. Didn't really think about it. *(Reassuring himself)* But that is a good thing. It's a good thing, no it's not a good thing it's a great thing. I think she's been waiting for me to ask her, she didn't have to think up the answer because she already knew what she was going to say, and to say no was never in the equation? She was always going to say yes. But sometimes it's easier to say yes. (*Deflated and beginning to question his actions*) Much more convenient to say yes, to say no is just too hard. To say yes is the easier option, an easier way to get out of things.

(*DAN jumps off the chair and stands next to it. He is now plagued by a worry that Beth isn't interested. He takes off his suit jacket and puts it neatly over the back of the chair.*)

That would be the problem. That she didn't think about it. There was no pause in her voice. It was yes straight away, no thinking time. She forgot how to say no, it was just a knee jerk response. (*DAN pauses and folds his arms*) I've worked with her for the past six weeks and she hasn't asked me out yet. She never bothered to ask me if I wanted to meet away from work, go for a drink or a coffee away from the office. She didn't come up and ask me. There is a reason to why people don't ask you to meet them away from work. It's because they don't want to see you away from work. (*Assuring himself*) She does always talk to me at Friday meetings, we always have a talk about the week and what we are going to do over the weekend. (*Angry to himself*) Ever heard of just being polite, not wanting to be rude and wanting to be part of the conversation? What else is she going to do? Just stand there like a stunned dummy when I talk to her?

(*DAN sits down on the chair, his level of doubt is ever increasing.*)

She's so pretty, she has the most beautiful face. And let's be frank, gorgeous girls have never particularly gone for me. Girls with beautiful faces don't go for boring accountant eggheads who enjoy playing golf. And I'm not even very good at golf. I have a handicap of nineteen. You can't really get much worse. I still can't hit a five wood straight. I've put a girl in an awkward position. I basically forced her to come on a date with me. She had to say yes, she's far too polite; to say no was never an option. I didn't leave her with any other options. It's so much easier to say yes. Beth is such a nice girl, she probably saw my pathetic happy face and she didn't want to hurt me. Beth knew that if she said no, that it would hurt me. Put me in a sad disappointed mood. *(DAN takes a deep breathe)* She's probably conjuring up excuses now to why she can't come. Too much work to catch up on, she has to stay back and prepare things for the up coming half yearly accounts report. Or maybe it will be her sister's birthday and that she is sorry she just completely forgot? I don't blame her; I don't blame her at all.

(DAN gets off the chair and loosens his tie and rolls up his sleeves and sits on the floor near the chair; he is now full of doubt and has decided that Beth doesn't really want to go out with him.)

I guess I should have thought first, I never think enough. That's my problem, I don't think. I just jump into things. I don't evaluate the consequences. I just run in and say things. I need to think things through, make sure that I am not ruining things for people. I shouldn't get any big ideas because they don't get me anywhere. I'll have to think up something so I can cancel. The least I can do is not make her stress out thinking up a plausible excuse. I need to think up something, something to get me out of it.

(DAN pauses for a moment.)

I'll have the flu. I'll ring her up, take the day off work because I have the flu and I don't want to give anyone else a cold. That way I wouldn't have to be at work and it wouldn't come up in conversation thus avoiding a really awkward moment. It saves her the hassle if I come up with an excuse. I wish she had said no, just easier if she would have said no. I wish she would have just said no.

(DAN gets up off the floor, gets his jacket off the seat, tucks it under his arm and walks deflated off the stage.)

The End

Notes on Contributors

Jeffrey Alfier has work appearing or forthcoming in *Connecticut Review*, *Tulane Review*, and *South Carolina Review*. His latest chapbook is *The City Without Her* (Kindred Spirit Press, 2012), and his first full-length book of poems, *The Wolf Yearling*, is forthcoming from Pecan Grove Press.

Devreaux Baker is a 2011 recipient of the PEN Oakland/Josephine Miles Poetry Award for her book *Red Willow People*. She is a 2012 recipient of the Hawaii Council on Humanities International Poetry award, and has received a MacDowell Fellowship, a Hawthornden Castle Fellowship, 3 California Arts Council Awards, and the Helene Wurlitzer Foundation Fellowship. She has published three books of poetry: *Light at the Edge*, *Beyond the Circumstance of Sight* and *Red Willow People*. She was an editor of *Wood, Water, Air and Fire: The Anthology of Mendocino Women Writers* and producer of *The Voyagers:Original Student Writing* for KZYX. (See www.devreauxbaker.com.)

Sue Booker lives, writes and paints in Sydney, if not necessarily in that order. Her short fiction has appeared in *Meanjin*, *Escape* (Spineless Wonders) and *Encounters: Modern Australian Short Stories* (ed. Barry Oakley). Her long fiction has attracted mentorships from Varuna and the Australian Society of Authors. Her in-between-length fiction is currently under construction.

Andrew Burke is an Australian poet who moved from Perth to Corowa, NSW, in 2012. His current titles include *Undercover of Lightness: New & Selected Poems* (Walleah Press, Hobart, 2012), *QWERTY* (Mulla Mulla Press, Kalgoorlie, 2011), and *Shikibu Shuffle* in collaboration with Phil Hall (above / ground press, Ontario, 2012). He is represented in *The Best Australian Poems 2012*, ed John Tranter, (Black Inc., 2012). In his spare time, Burke is a talent scout for Regime on the eastern seaboard. Read his daily posts at hispirits.blogspot.com.

Ashley Capes teaches Media and English in Victoria, Australia. His first collection of poetry *pollen and the storm* was published with the assistance of Small Change Press in 2008, and his second collection *Stepping Over Seasons* was released by Interactive Press in 2009. A haiku chapbook *Orion Tips the Saucepan* was released by Picaro Press in 2010. His most recent release will be his third poetry collection *between giants* to be released by Ginninderra Press in 2012. His work can be found in a variety of print and online publications in Australia (and even once exhibited on public transport in Melbourne) and a few overseas. He has worked in community arts where he assisted with exhibitions, organised short story competitions and poetry gigs, and in music retail while completing a double degree in Arts/Education at Monash University. Recently his work has been awarded a commendation in the Rosemary Dobson Poetry Prize and in 2009 he won the Ipswich Open Poetry Award with the poem 'shell.'

Mikaela Castledine I am a writer and an artist, born in the Western Australian wheatbelt, living in the Perth Hills. I had my first poem published when I was fifteen and a short story published in *Indigo* in 2011. In the intervening 32 years I have studied applied science and interior design, have grown my arts practice, grown two children to adulthood and have continued always to write. In the last 12 months I have had poetry, short stories and creative non fiction commended in a variety of writing competitions. I am currently studying for my Masters in Creative Writing and Literature at Deakin University as well as crocheting crows for a major sculpture exhibition. Much of my creative work can be found at: mikaelacastledine.wordpress.com

2012 Café Poet at Open Studio, Northcote, through Australian Poetry, **Sofia Chapman** studied Modern Languages at University in Tasmania, then took up the accordion and has performed in Europe, Britain, NZ, New Caledonia and the U.S. Her poems have been published in *Prelude* and *Inscribe*, and her plays include *The Anorexic Chef* and *The Accidental Death of an Accordionist* (performed at La Mama) and *Desperate Gallery* (Short & Sweet Festival). Her epic *The Four Accordionists of the Apocalypse* won the 'Best Emerging Writer' award at the 2012 Melbourne Fringe Festival.

Robbie Coburn was born in country Victoria, where he still resides. His first chapbook of poems *Human Batteries* was published by Picaro Press in 2012. He is currently working on a book for children, a verse novel and a volume of memoir called *Years of Skin*. Robbie's personal website is robbiecoburn.com. Robbie's poem, 'There Are No Strangers', was published in *Regime 01*.

Tobi Cogswell is a three-time Pushcart nominee and a Best of the Net nominee. Credits include or are forthcoming in various journals in the US, UK, Sweden and Australia. Her fifth and latest chapbook is *Lit Up*, (Kindred Spirit Press). She is the co-editor of *San Pedro River Review* (www.sprreview.com).

Gary Colombo De Piazzi is an emerging Western Australian poet who originally dabbled in poetry in 2002 for cathartic reasons. The sense of liberation and creative joy captured his interest and instilled a desire to explore the power and wonder of words. Whilst he has dabbled with traditional forms of poetry he prefers the freedom of free verse and loves to write purely from the heart without constraints of form and syntax, to mix and mesh words to draw an emotion, raise a point. His poetry has been published in various Western Australian and Australian anthologies and web based journals. He was a featured poet at the 2009 WA Spring Poetry Festival and joint winner of the 2009 Creatrix Haiku Prize and winner of the inaugural Bodhi Tree Bookstore Haiku competition in 2010. He has received commendations in the 2011 Fremantle Press Tanka competition and the 2011 & 2012 Creatrix Haiku and Poetry Prizes. Gary's love for nature is reflected in his poetry and photographs. In 2008 his book *The Pinnacles, A Natural Experience*, a collection of photographs and poems exploring various experiences with nature and featuring the Pinnacles Desert at Cervantes was published. He is retired and divides his time between his writing, family, voluntary positions on committees and exploring the elusive moments of haiku.

Jake Davies is a post-graduate student at the University of Sydney. His poetry has appeared in *Visible Ink* and *page seventeen* and he reviews on a semi-regular basis for *artsHub*.

Jim Davis has been a 'scribbler' for some time and has had a couple of poems published in *The Fremantle Herald*. He has had an ambition to produce a volume of work in different literary genres; non-fiction, poetry, drama and fiction. So far a longer work of fiction escapes him. His drama writing includes melodrama, a full length 'kitchen sink' drama and the postscript to Shakespeare's 'Romeo and Juliet' about the possible trial of Friar Lawrence. The non-fiction was a self published memoir of his time teaching in the Arabian Gulf at the time of the invasion of Afghanistan and the second Iraq war titled *Stories from Arabia*. The volume of poetry was also self published and titled *The Straw Sandal Traveller*.

Paul Fauteux received his MFA from George Mason University, where he was the 2011-2012 Completion Fellow. His recent work has appeared or is forthcoming in *Fat City Review* and *Sugar Mule*, for the advocacy of other fine poets on *The Lit Pub*, and his first chapbook, *The Best Way to Drink Tea*, is out from Plan B Press. *How to Un-do Things*, a book-length manuscript, was recognized as a semi-finalist in the 11th Annual Slope Editions Book Prize.

Michelle Faye currently resides in Mount Lawley, Western Australia and is completing a Bachelor of Arts in English and Creative Writing at Murdoch University. A writer of poetry and short stories, she is due to be published in the upcoming WA Poets Inc Love Poems for Valentine's Day 2013 anthology. Her short story 'Father' was recently shortlisted and received a commendation for the Katharine Susannah Prichard 2012 Short Fiction Awards.

Benito Di Fonzo was born into an Irish-Italian working class family in Sydney's Inner West. Journalist, playwright, poet and performer Benito Di Fonzo has written for, and been profiled by, the best and worst of publications including *The Sydney Morning Herald*, *The Sun Herald*, *The Australian*, *CNN*, and *Bardfly Magazine* (where he was editor). Benito co-hosted Sydney's premier poetry and spoken word night for a decade and has performed his narrative neo-beat poems and spoken word in London, Edinburgh, Sydney, Melbourne, Rome, Adelaide, Perth and Indonesia. As well as writing radio serials and plays for 2SER and 2FBI he has had two plays broadcast live from The Sydney Opera House. He has also performed on ABC 702 & Radio National, 3RRR (Melbourne) and Resonance FM (UK) amongst others. In 2005 Independence Jones Guerrilla Press published Benito's free-verse novel *Her, Leaving, As the Acid Hits* to positive reviews. His debut stage play *Breakfast At Krishna's* filled houses at Tap, Sydney in 2000. Benito's 2010 production *The Chronic Ills of Robert Zimmerman, AKA Bob Dylan (A Lie)* was a hit of Adelaide Fringe before several sold-out seasons in Sydney and a litany of glowing reviews, resulting in the show being awarded Best of Independent Theatre 2010. It has since toured regionally and been adapted in a verse-novel available through Amazon. Benito's second Fonzo Journalistic show, *Lenny Bruce: 13 Daze Un-Dug in Sydney 1962* will premiere in 2013. Benito achieved degrees in Literature and Creative Writing at The University of Western Sydney and has done postgraduate studies at AFTRS, Sydney University and UTS. In 2001 he was awarded the Inner City Life Literary Award by The NSW Writers' Centre. His favourite colour is irrelevant.

Jonathan Greenhaus Twice-nominated for the Pushcart, I was a runner-up in the 2012 Georgetown Review Prize and am the author of a chapbook, *Sebastian's Relativity* (Anobium Books). My poems have appeared or are forthcoming in *The Believer, The Bitter Oleander, Going Down Swinging, JAAM,* and *Other Poetry,* among others, and two of my poems are featured in the just-released anthology *New Sun Rising: Stories for Japan.*

Jonathan Hadwen is a Brisbane poet. He has been published in *Westerly, Stand Magazine, Southerly, Page Seventeen, Cordite,* and *foam:e* as well as other publications in Australia and overseas. In 2010, his micro-collection *Night Swim* was published in volume one of the Brisbane New Voices series. He has appeared on the programs for the Queensland Poetry Festival and the Woodford Folk Festival, and has read his poetry on 4ZZZ local radio.

Nathan Hondros is a writer, poet and publisher. He has had a number of incarnations, but is getting close to nirvana at Regime Books, where he is one of the editors of *Regime Magazine.* His work has appeared in *Westerly, The Australian, Masthead, The Drunken Boat* and many other magazines and journals. The Australian Broadcasting Corporation has adapted his work into radio plays. He wrote and published *Man and Beast,* a collection of short stories, with his good mate Damon Lockwood in 2009.

Kenneth Hudson has been published in national and international journals.

Kathryn Hummel's fiction, non-fiction and poetry has appeared in Australia, New Zealand, the US, Nepal, Bangladesh, and India in anthologies and publications including *Meanjin, M/C Journal, Social Alternatives, Himal Southasian* and *PopMatters*. Recently she has completed a major piece of narrative ethnography, drawing on her experiences of life and work in Bangladesh, as part of a PhD in Social Sciences at the University of South Australia. Kathryn was a writer in residence in 2011 for Australian Poetry's Café Poet Program.

Rose Hunter is an Australian living in Mexico. Her book of poetry, *[four paths]*, was published by Texture Press (Oklahoma, 2012), and her book, *to the river* (also poetry), was published by Artistically Declined Press (Oregon, 2010). Links to more of her writing can be found at *Whoever Brought Me Here Will Have To Take Me Home* (roseh400. wordpress.com). She has appeared in journals such as *DIAGRAM, anderbo, Juked, Bluestem, PANK, Blip,* and *The Nervous Breakdown*. She tweets, @roseh400.

Andy Jackson's *Among the Regulars* (papertiger media, 2010) was shortlisted for the Kenneth Slessor Prize. His poems have recently appeared in *Meanjin, Cordite, Wordgathering, Medical Journal of Australia* and *Best Australian Poems 2012*. He is currently working on a series of poems exploring medical tourism, and a book of portrait poems of people with Marfan Syndrome. He blogs at amongtheregulars. wordpress.com.

Peter Jeffery OAM is heavily involved in Multicultural Art, Radio and Community Television and was recently Chair of WA Poetry Inc. He is returning to poetry after a long absence except for elegies for dear departed friends. He is hopeful of a collected verse anthology in the coming year.

Helga Jermy was born in Derbyshire, England, and now lives on the rural northwest coast of Tasmania where she works as a social worker and writes short stories and poetry. She has been previously published in *Regime 01* and online, including *Australian Poetry* poems of the week, and is working towards a first collection of poetry.

Erin Kelly is an environmental scientist who balances the cold scientific methodology of his professional life with the color and warmth of words and music. He is hungry and angry but not fat or mean. He likes storms at the end of a hot day and writes short stories while listening to 90's rock. Erin's work has a home at *Word Riot*, *Vibewire*, *Flash Fiction Offensive*, *Zinewest* and *Hypallage*.

Teri Louise Kelly is the author of three published memoirs and one poetry collection. Her short stories and poems have appeared nationally and internationally. She has also released a spoken word CD & in 2013 is due to release a further three volumes of poetry and a memoir based on her experience of changing gender. An average bass player in an average band she currently resides in Adelaide, South Australia.

Rosalee Kiely was born in Melbourne, Australia, and completed Australian Literature Honours at the University of Sydney. Her poetry has been published in *Voiceworks* and *dotdotdash*. She currently studies Spanish language in Mexico.

After seven years of newspaper, online and broadcast reporting **Elise Kinsella** has thrown out her style guides and started writing entirely fictional stories. She hopes to continue telling stories that are true and stories that are the inventions of her mad, mad imaginings.

Mark Konik is a writer from Newcastle, Australia. He has had plays performed and published in Australia, The United Kingdom, The United States, New Zealand and India. His plays have been presented at the Adelaide and Sydney Fringe Festivals and he has received commissions from Scenepool Productions (London). His short film 'Making Toast with You' has just been filmed and produced in Los Angeles. To contact the author please email markkonik@hotmail.com.

Christopher Konrad lives and works in Western Australia. He has a PhD in creative writing and has had poems published in many journals such as *Westerly*, *WetInk*, *Page 17*, *Staples*, *Indigo* and in the online publications *Creatrix*, *Island*, *Swamp* and *Perigee* (US). Co-authored an anthology with two other poets, *Sandfire* (2012), published by Sunline Press. First Prize Tom Collins Poetry Prize, 2009 and Todhunter Literary Award, 2012. www.writingwa.org/membership/ckonrad. www.wapoets.net.au/documents/poets/ChristopherKonrad/

Roland Leach is the proprietor of Sunline Press, which has published fifteen collections of poetry by Australian poets. He has three collections of poetry, the latest *My Father's Pigs* published by Picaro Press. He is a past winner of the Newcastle Poetry Prize and Josephine Ulrick Prize and was the recipient of an Australia Council Grant to write poetry in the Galapagos Islands.

Damon Lockwood has been writing professionally for over ten years and has had his work produced all across the country. He won the national *Write Now!* 2005 competition for Best Script with his one-man show *Domestic Bliss* and his script *Pri-mates*, for Barking Gecko Theatre Company, was published in *The Australian Script Centre Collection #6*. *Nature as Explained by Theatre*, for Longwood Productions, was chosen as the *Play of the Month* for the Australian Script Centre. Other scripts include *Muttaburrasaurus* (Spare Parts Puppet Theatre), *Gogo Fish: The Fossil that Changed the World* (Barking Gecko Theatre Company), *12:15, Saturday Night* (Damage Theatre) and *A Change in the Weather*. Recent productions include *Horsehead*, *Short Four Play*, and *I (Honestly) Love You*, all for Longwood Productions. Damon completed a year's mentorship with *Spare Parts Puppet Theatre* in 2005, and completed a co-production with *Deckchair Theatre Company* in October 2009 with two new scripts, *Forget-Me-Not* and *Refractions*. He has released a book of short stories with fellow West Aussie writer Nathan Hondros entitled *Man and Beast*. He currently holds the position of Literature Manager with *Black Swan State Theatre Company*.

Shane McCauley has been a TAFE/University lecturer since the mid-1970s and seven of his books of poetry have been published, most recently *The Drunken Elk* (Sunline Press, 2010) and *Ghost Catcher* (Studio Press, 2012). He was awarded the 2008 Max Harris Poetry Award. He runs a fortnightly poetry workshop for the OOTA Writers' Group at the Fremantle Arts Centre.

A seven-time Pushcart-Prize nominee and National Park Artist-in-Residence, **Karla Linn Merrifield** has had nearly 300 poems appear in dozens of journals and anthologies. She has eight books to her credit, the newest of which are *The Ice Decides: Poems of Antarctica* (Finishing Line Press) and *Liberty's Vigil, The Occupy Anthology: 99 Poets among the 99%*, which she co-edited. Forthcoming from Salmon Poetry is

Athabaskan Fractal and Other Poems of the Far North. Her *Godwit: Poems of Canada* (FootHills) received the 2009 Eiseman Award for Poetry and she recently received the Dr. Sherwin Howard Award for the best poetry published in *Weber — The Contemporary West* in 2012. She is assistant editor and poetry book reviewer for *The Centrifugal Eye* (www.centrifugaleye.com). Visit her blog, *Vagabond Poet*, at http://karlalinn.blogspot.com.

Carly-Jay Metcalfe is a Brisbane based writer of poetry, literary fiction, memoir and biography. Her work has appeared in *Overland*, *Cordite Poetry Journal*, *Stylus Poetry Journal* and maintains a blog at www.bruisesyoucantouch.com

Kate Middleton is the author of *Fire Season* (Giramondo, 2009), awarded the WA Premier's Award for Poetry in 2009. From September 2011 — September 2012 she was the inaugural Sydney City Poet.

Originally from New Zealand **Carol Millner** is now based in Perth. Sixteen pages of her poetry were published in *Amber Contains the Sun* (Funded through DCA, A Few New Words, 2008). Her short stories have won awards and been published in anthologies (*Lines in the Sand*, FAWWA, 2008) and journals such as *indigo* (Summer 2009). 'Under the Jacaranda' was commended in the Glen Phillips Poetry Prize (Peter Cowan Writers' Centre, 2012).

Norm Neill's poetry has appeared in journals, including *Five Bells*, *Blue Dog* and *Social Alternatives*, and in four edited anthologies. His poem 'Post-industrial' appeared in the *Sun-Herald* newspaper in 2011. The Robin Gibson Gallery exhibited sixteen of his poems responding to paintings in 2010. His poem 'World Cup Final' came second in the 2009 Inner City Life competition and 900 Days was commended in 2011. In 2012, Norm read his poetry at the Sydney Writers' and Newtown Festivals and read as featured poet at the PoetryUnlimited reading at the Harold Park Hotel. He is convenor of the weekly Wednesday Night Poets workshop at the NSW Writers' Centre. He has had two non-fiction works published, as well as more than 740 letters in broadsheet newspapers.

Rodney Nelson's work began appearing in mainstream journals long ago; but he turned to fiction and did not write a poem for twenty-two years, restarting in the 2000s. So he is both older and 'new.' See his page in the Poets & Writers directory http://www.pw.org/content/rodney_nelson for a notion of the publishing history. He has worked as a copy editor in the Southwest and now lives in the northern Great Plains. Recently, his poem 'One Winter' won a Poetry Kit Award for 2011 (U.K.); it had appeared in *Symmetry Pebbles*. His 'Upstream in Idaho' received a Best of Issue Award at the late Neon Beam (also England). The chapbook *Metacowboy* was published in 2011; another title, *In Wait*, in November 2012.

Ian Nichols is one of Australia's best known unknown writers, since he has written well over 2,500 book reviews and articles for *The West Australian* newspaper, is one of the editorial collective for *Andromeda Spaceways In-flight Magazine* (and a founding member), has been nominated for Aurealis, Ditmar and Tin Duck awards, winning one of the latter, and, along the way, has had a novel, a book of poetry, a book on Shakespeare and a dozen or so short stories published, both in Australia and internationally. Born in Wales an awfully long time ago, he was brought to Australia in 1950 and had the remarkable good sense to stay. Educated at seven different universities in the halcyon days when such things were free, he now has a doctorate in that most useless of areas, creative writing. He has been an actor, factory worker, psych nurse, etc, but mostly a teacher god save his soul. Married, with an adult stepson and a dog, you can buy him a drink, preferably Glen Ord, since he's now officially a starving writer.

Graham Nunn is a Queensland poet whose fifth collection of poetry, *Ocean Hearted* was released in 2010. His publications include:
- *A Zen Firecracker – selected haiku* (Impressed Publishing, Brisbane, 2003)
- *Share the Tragedy* (Impressed Publishing, Brisbane, 2004)
- *Measuring the Depth* (Pardalote Press, Hobart, 2005)
- *Ruined Man* (Small Change Press, Brisbane, 2007)
- *Ocean Hearted* (Another Lost Shark Publications, Brisbane, 2010)

Brennan O'Shea lives and works in a seaside suburb of Adelaide and has had stories published in print and on-line (including *Skive Magazine, FourWNineteen, LiNQ,* and *Imago*. His story 'The Wolf and Peter' appeared in the Wirra Wirra Vineyards Anthology, *Goodnight goodnight* in 2009.

Ryan O'Neill's short stories have appeared in numerous journals and anthologies. His latest collection, *The Weight of a Human Heart* was shortlisted for the 2012 Queensland Literary Awards.

Fikret Pajalic came to Melbourne as a refugee in 1994. He has a BA Photography from RMIT and for years he used images to convey a message, only to realise that some stories are best told in words. He won equal first prize at the 2011 Ada Cambridge Short Story prize, has been highly commended in the 2011 Grace Marion VWC Emerging Writers Competition and in the 2011 Brimbank Short Story Awards. His work has been published in *Platform* and *Hypallage* magazines and the upcoming *Wordsmiths of Melton Anthology*. Fikret can be contacted at pajalic@iprimus.com.au.

Geoff Page, b.1940, is a Canberra-based poet who has published twenty collections of poetry as well as two novels, five verse novels and several other works including anthologies, translations and a biography of the jazz musician, Bernie McGann. His awards including the Grace Leven Prize, the Christopher Brennan Award, the Queensland Premier's Prize for Poetry and the 2001 Patrick White Literary Award. He has read his work and talked on Australian poetry throughout Europe as well as in India, Singapore, China, Korea, the United States and New Zealand. His recent books include:
- *Lawrie & Shirley:The Final Cadenza:A Movie in Verse* (Pandanus Books, 2007)
- *60 Classic Australian Poems* (UNSW Press, 2009)
- *A Sudden Sentence in the Air: Jazz Poems* (Extempore, 2011)
- *Coda for Shirley* (Interactive Press, 2011)
- *Cloudy Nouns* (Picaro Press, 2012)
- *1953* (forthcoming University of Queensland Press, 2013)
- *New Selected Poems* (Puncher & Wattmann, 2013)

More information: www.geoffpagepoet.com.au.

Chris Palazzolo is a novelist, poet and video store clerk who lives in Perth, Western Australia, with his wife and two children. His short story, 'Appointment with an Orphic Headhunter', was published in *Regime 01*.

Richard King Perkins II is a state-sponsored advocate for residents in long-term care facilities. He has a wife, Vickie and a daughter, Sage. His work has appeared in hundreds of publications including *Prime Mincer*, *Sheepshead Review*, *Sierra Nevada Review*, *Imago*, *Prairie Winds* and *The Red Cedar Review*.

Glen Phillips is a Western Australian writer and Honorary Professor of English and Writing at Edith Cowan University. He is Patron of the Katherine Susannah Prichard Writers Centre, has published 14 collections of poetry, including *Spring Burning* (Salt Publishing, 1999) and has edited anthologies, critical works and textbooks. Glen's poems have been published in more than 50 anthologies, journals and newspapers in Australia, Asia, America and Italy and he has read poetry to audiences at festivals or conferences in most Australian state capitals and in towns all over his home state of WA. He has been invited to read poetry at Cambridge University (UK) and Kenyon College (Ohio), and at universities in Italy, Spain, Denmark, China, India, Thailand and Singapore. His poems have been screened on ABCTV and SBS and regional TV networks. Glen's poetry has been broadcast on the ABC radio, and on commercial and regional stations. It has been included in the ABC's Poetica program in 2006, 2007 and 2009. His jointly written collection of poems *Singing Granites* (with British poet Anne Born) also appeared in 2008 and his *Shanghai Suite and Other Poems* was published in 2009. In 2009 he also published *Red Shift Cosmology: 42 Name Day Poems* and in 2011 *A Show of Colours and Intersections*. In 2012 his bilingual (with Chinese translations) *Six Seasons* and *The Woman River* were published in north and south China respectively. He is writing a trilogy of novellas based in Shanghai and has a new collection of poetry appearing with Salt Publishing in the UK later in 2012. Three other volumes of poetry are in preparation as well as a collection of 24 short stories.

Charles Pitter has a degree in English and French literature from Middlesex and Paris VIII Universities. He has written for a number of different magazines and journals and has been nominated for a Puchcart Prize. His website is http://charlespitter.com/ and a chapbook of his poetry is available from Fire Hazard Press.

Frederick Pollack Author of two book-length narrative poems, *The Adventure* and *Happiness*, both published by Story Line Press. Other poems in print and online journals. Adjunct professor creative writing George Washington University.

Miro Sandev is a poet, short fiction writer and reviewer, based in Sydney. His poems have appeared in the *Red Room Disappearing, Hypallage* and *Dissent*. He reviews theatre and literature for *ArtsHub*. His essays have appeared in *Arena Magazine* and *New Matilda*.

Petri Ivalo Sinda's previous publications include a novelette in the inaugural volume of *Daikaiju!*, a cyberpunk story in the late online publication *Overland Express*, a Mark Leyner-ish surreal comedy in *Paper Radio*, as well as a story in the inaugural issue of *Regime*. 'Meltdown Express' was inspired by his first continental road run to Sydney. In 2012 Petri relocated from Perth to Melbourne where he failed to die of cappuccino poisoning. Now his ambitions revolve around something known as alcohol.

Barnaby Smith is a writer, journalist and musician based in Sydney's inner west. After a childhood in the rural Hawkesbury he lived in Europe for many years before returning to Australia in 2010. His poetry has appeared in *Southerly, Wet Ink, Regime* and *Prole*.

Ian C Smith's work has appeared in *Axon: Creative Explorations, The Best Australian Poetry, Chiron Review, Island, Southerly,* and *Westerly.* His fifth book is *Contains Language*, Ginninderra Press (Adelaide). He lives in the Gippsland Lakes area of Victoria, Australia.

Joanna Wolthuizen was born in Melbourne, Victoria and currently lives in Sydney, New South Wales. She is an artist and writer of short fiction and poetry. Joanna exhibits frequently in Sydney and Melbourne, and her paintings have been included in numerous national award exhibitions. Joanna's artworks are held in private and corporate collections throughout Australia.

Regime de Vivre Poetry Prize 2013

We at Regime Books would like to set the poets of the world an interesting challenge. The *Regime de Vivre Poetry Prize 2013* will be awarded to the poem that the judges consider has best reflected the spirit of the prize itself.

To understand the spirit of the prize, we hand you the following clues, which if properly pursued will reveal everything you need to know:

- The title of the prize is in itself a clue; and
- A maxim attributed by Samuel Beckett to Sébastien Chamfort, but which is actually a fragment from Blaise Pascal: *'Que le coeur de l'homme est creux et plein d'ordure'**.

In addition to a warm inner glow (or a sense of existential emptiness, as the case may be), the winner shall be awarded US$200 and be published in the third edition of Regime Magazine. Two runners-up will be awarded US$50, along with publication.

Poems must be less than 30 lines in length and unpublished. A non-refundable entry fee of US$10 for each poem will be levied. Entries will not be considered from those directly associated with Regime Books or Regime Magazine. Any money raised above the amount of the cash prize will be used to help with the publishing costs of Regime Magazine. No correspondence will be entered into and the judges' decision will be final.

Deadline for entries is strictly Midnight EST, 31 March 2013. The winners will be announced by 30 April 2013.

Entries will only be accepted online at: regime.submittable.com

For more information visit: regimebooks.com.au

* A handy translation is 'How hollow and full of ribaldry is the heart of man!'